UNLAWFUL ENTRY

Further Titles by Jo Bannister from Severn House

AN UNCERTAIN DEATH

UNLAWFUL ENTRY

Jo Bannister

This title first published in Great Britain 1998 by
SEVERN HOUSE PUBLISHERS LTD of
9–15 High Street, Sutton, Surrey SM1 1DF.
Originally published in 1988 under the title
of *The Mason Codex*.
First published in the USA 1998 by
SEVERN HOUSE PUBLISHERS INC., of
595 Madison Avenue, New York, NY 10022.

British Library Cataloguing in Publication Data

Bannister, Jo
     Unlawful entry
     1.   Illegal aliens – United States – Fiction
     2.   Mexico – Emigration and immigration – Fiction
     3.   Thrillers
     1. Title
     823.9'14 [F]

     ISBN 0-7278-5359-7

Printed and bound in Great Britain by
MPG Books Ltd, Bodmin, Cornwall.

Cristóbal

1

My brother still hadn't fixed the hole in his exhaust so I knew it was him even before the car pulled up at my gate. Also, the dogs barked. They don't usually bark at strangers, only at family.

I swung my legs off the bed and groped for my dressing-gown, wondering what time it was. The grandfather downstairs had just struck twelve but it wasn't all that good a guide, if the humidity wasn't right it could lose or gain whole days. The Woolworths travel alarm was more reliable, if people didn't pile up the books on the shelf in front of it. I moved three sombre treatises on ancient history and a well-thumbed paperback of low humour – confiscated from an inattentive 3b but thumbed mostly by me, not him – and the clock said it was 11.30.

It was not an inordinately strange time for David to come round – our working-hours were more comp- lementary than concurrent, and the middle of the night was about the only time either could be sure of catching the other – but I was troubled when I heard his key in the lock. His custom, particularly at night, was to do me the courtesy of ringing my bell. Departure from that practice meant that he had something other than my putative love-life on his mind.

We met on the stairs. One look at his face quelled whatever inclination I felt to tell him I was entertaining three British Lions and a Wallaby: he was in no state for jokes. He looked shocked – literally, his face white, the skin

5

drawn pale and clammy over the broad bones, his eyes stretched and somehow hollow.

My first thought was for his wife and daughters. 'David, in God's name, what's happened?'

He drew a deep breath, his head with its schoolboy mop of straw-coloured hair rocking back. The movement seemed to leach some of the tension from him. His eyes seemed to see me again: bright blue eyes, our mother's eyes, the blue of a summer sky over Snowdon. But he had our father's build, somewhere between a scrum half and Caernarvon Castle; if he had never had our father's strength of mind or of purpose, he was a great deal easier to like.

He wiped one hand across his face, essayed a feeble smile and retreated down the stairs into the living-room. 'I need a drink.'

I didn't ask what. I poured him three fat fingers of Scotch and said, with what I considered commendable restraint in the circumstances, 'And I need an explanation.'

But he wasn't quite ready. It took a few minutes of just sitting there quietly, in his raincoat because he hadn't got round to taking it off, and another fistful of whisky before he had sufficient command of his thoughts and his nerves and whatever hags were riding him to tell me what had happened. Even at that he had to go way back to make sense of it – for me, but mainly for him.

The old man was a professional seaman most of his adult life, and indeed some of his boyhood, for he first shipped at the age of fourteen and his earliest voyages were in sail. He was very proud of that, although in truth by the time he was starting the days of the deep-sea commercial square-rigger were already history and the only sailing ships still beating their way into the Pacific around the killing rocks of Cape Horn were school ships, subsidised by the great steamer companies as a training-ground for officers.

He loved all his ships, prestigious and fast and beautiful and otherwise, but for those first great sailing ships, the last Cape Horners, he reserved a special, splendid passion. Three weeks before he died, at the age of eighty-four, he could hold you spellbound with his narrative of those apprentice passages: twice round the Horn, twice in the North Atlantic which could be just as bad, and once storming down the Roaring Forties to Newcastle in Australia and then on across the Pacific to California. He left his last sailing-ship in San Francisco, transferred on promotion to a steamer, but almost seventy years later he could take you on a guided tour of every mast he had climbed – three each on the two barques and four on the barquentine – with the sails, rigging, trim and characteristics of each, whether they were wet or dry, ladies or mankillers.

Then came the first of his three strokes, that robbed him of that magical, hypnotic, intense ability to communicate, so that the remaining brilliance of his spirit was held captive behind bewildered eyes. The second stroke took the strength from his limbs and the third, only days later, played the gentleman and killed him, setting his soul free of his ruined body to sail the deep waters with the ghosts of his gull-winged ships. I missed him.

David was his executor. He was the obvious choice – the son, the eldest child, the accountant. All the same, it would have been better if our father had named me, because I would have coped better with the old bastard's last bombshell.

The will was in fact executed and the estate disposed some months earlier, so when David got the message from the family solicitor to call on him as soon as possible, inside or outside office hours, he couldn't imagine why. He presumed, being a worrier, that something had gone badly wrong and he had distributed funds which did not properly belong to the estate; he was mentally assessing how much could be got back without recourse to civil war when Mr Arkwright's secretary, who had thought her employer had left until David gave his name, showed him into the office.

Neither Arkwright's expression, nor his opening words, nor the rattle of teacups in the outer office, gave my brother any reason to believe he was being overly pessimistic.

'Mr Meredith, I have some strange news for you. I think you should prepare yourself for a shock.'

So David sat down and steeled himself, and Mr Arkwright told him about our father's other son – the one neither David nor I had any knowledge of, the one he sired on some Mexican girl about the time he and my mother were celebrating their silver wedding.

The one who, eight days before, had been found dead in the back of a lorry, one of seven wetbacks who died of cold and no air in a sealed trailer abandoned in the upland wilderness of Texas by smugglers who took their money and left them to a death as certain as, if slower than, any delivered by a gun.

His name had been Cristóbal Baez, and he had been twenty-seven years old.

Mr Arkwright, it transpired, had known of his existence before. Señorita Baez, apparently, was the daughter of a good family who would not countenance her raising a half-caste bastard. At a few weeks the infant was farmed out to foster parents and the bill was forwarded to my father. His solicitor arranged for the payments to be made out of a trust fund of which my mother could remain ignorant. Later the boy was in trouble on both sides of the border, and the old man bought him out of it. He wound up the trust when Cristóbal turned twenty-one. He was a citizen of Mexico who had lived illegally in the United States, been deported and was trying to get back when, due to some hitch or glitch or perhaps just remembering urgent business elsewhere, the driver they had hired unhitched his rig from the sealed trailer and drove off into the sunset, leaving his live cargo to the bitter chill of a desert winter night.

None of them survived. When the trailer was eventually found and opened, among my brother's meagre effects was the six-year-old letter from Mr Arkwright that was his last contact with his father. Conceived in error, born in shame, he had lived in poverty and died of mere expediency. He had had twenty-seven years and not a lot of luck.

Mr Arkwright, apparently, deliberated for half a day about what he should properly do with the information he had received from the Texas authorities. Finally he decided he had no right to keep it from the effective, if unconscious, next-of-kin and called David's office.

We seemed to sit for a long time, David and I, not looking at one another, not talking. At one point I got up and made some coffee. David ignored it, working his way steadily, with a kind of savage deliberation and not much pleasure, through the whisky bottle. I couldn't tell what he was feeling. I couldn't have told him how I felt.

We had had a funny sort of family life, with my father at sea for much of the time all through our growing years. There had been little of him at home: not only in person but even symbolically – few pictures, fewer souvenirs. Even the rambling stone house belonged to my mother's family, and there was nothing in the atmosphere there that suggested anyone was missing. Yet when he came home on long, infrequent leaves he filled the place, a strange intense man who had been everywhere and done everything and clearly couldn't wait to be off and doing again. He appeared to have no interest in or affection for his children, and while he talked about his duty to his wife he clearly didn't actually feel much more of that. When he set off again with his two battered leather cases on the road to the station, there was a swing in his step that we never otherwise saw; and behind the rough warm stone of my mother's walls, his family breathed a sigh of relief too.

So life continued, its pleasant easy tenor occasionally interrupted as if by a burglar. In due course David married and moved out, though not far away, and I went up to university to read history and came back to teach it. I saw my father twice in those years, when our vacations unavoidably coincided, and on one of those occasions we fought.

My mother continued unaffected by the passage of time until the morning of the day she died, when she said she had a headache and was staying in bed, and I found her there still, quiet and cold, when I came in at four. My father flew home for the funeral, and flew back again four days later.

He was by now approaching seventy, though his owners thought he was sixty-four, and he had been master of his own ship for more than half his life. All the home he had recognised in those years had been a couple of connecting cabins on one carrier after another, and one of those his office.

One day, coming up through the Persian Gulf to take on oil at Kharg Island, someone pointed to some sea-snakes sliding over the slick surface, and he couldn't see them. Even with his binoculars he couldn't see them. He tried to focus on the jackstaff in the bows and couldn't. He couldn't see the coast of Qatar. He realised it had been months if not years since he had seen clearly over any distance. He knew his ship, he could read his charts and his instruments, he had good officers and a reliable crew – he had always had the ability to find and keep good crews. If, as seems likely, they knew he couldn't see worth a damn, they protected him – from the consequences and also from the knowledge.

He cared about them, too. When the ship docked he transferred his command to his first officer and took the first plane leaving for Europe. He never set foot on a ship again.

I had just grown used to living alone in my mother's

house that was now mine when he turned up with his two leather suitcases and his intense, faded green stare and moved in. He treated the house and me as if we belonged to him. He tried to banish my dogs to the yard. I threw my mother's will in his face. David walked into the middle of one particularly stormy exchange and, shocked at the violence of our feelings, tried to remonstrate with his father. The old man knocked him down. David never forgave him.

After that we reached an accommodation, a kind of armed neutrality; we never managed affection, even in his last days, but in time we fostered a somewhat reserved friendship. He was an interesting old sod when he wasn't just being an old sod. We talked about sailing-ships and strange lands and ancient peoples; we even talked quite a bit about Mexico. One of his ships sailed out of Veracruz and on leaves too brief to come to England he had seen many spectacular remnants of the pre-Columbian cultures which civilised meso-America.

We talked sometimes of going there together, but somehow never got round to it. Perhaps he was too conscious of the results of his own Mexican conquest to want to go back with me. About that time Cristóbal turned twenty-one and my father severed his last – indeed, it seemed almost his only – connection with his Mexican by-blow, the financial one. And I could see no other way of reading it than that lack of money had led him to the place where, six years later, he had died.

I looked round my lovely, lovely house, wondering what it was worth – the house and the furniture my grandfather had mostly got together, and his investments that were still one family's income, and David's business and his house, and both our cars, and all our foreign holidays – and how little of it would have served to keep our brother Cristóbal off a mortuary slab. If we had known. If our father had thought enough of any one of us to tell us.

David mumbled, savagely, out of the depths of his glass, 'How could he do that?'

I presumed he was thinking much the same as I was. The thick bitterness in his voice echoed that in my breast, a thick hard band that bit burning into my chest as I breathed. I answered him not because I knew the answers but because of the urgent need in me to seek some, because if I couldn't make some sense of what had happened soon that hard constriction in my chest was going to break something, possibly my heart. 'I don't know, David. But there had to be a reason. He wasn't a cruel man, not deliberately. You think maybe he just didn't know?'

David looked up slowly from his drink. The whisky made him move like a man under water – it was already clear he would be spending the night here, I'd have to phone Jan soon to stop her worrying – but had done nothing to soften the anger in his face. His eyes were dark with the thing akin to hatred which I had not seen there since the old man died. 'What?'

'Maybe he didn't know. It's possible – they hardly knew each other. Did they even write? There was nothing between them except a kind of accident – '

'Accident?' David snorted, slopping alcohol over his knee. 'You mean one day in down-town Veracruz he tripped and fell, and landed on some Mexican bint who'd just done the same thing? – so while they were down there they thought they'd just have a quick screw – ?'

He hadn't been thinking the same as me. He was filled with shock and resentment for an act of infidelity that had happened twenty-eight years ago and six thousand miles away, that had never until now touched our family, that had probably had no greater significance than the scratching of an itch by a restless man temporarily deprived of the responsibility for his ship at sea. But for the accident of conception there would have been nothing to tell, a brief silliness by a man already past middle age who had at least had the sense to indulge himself half a world away from his own doorstep. It might not have been admirable behaviour, but nor had it been a monstrous betrayal. Yet it was that brief and ancient sin which was feeding my brother's rage: the careless creation of an unsanctioned life, not the calculated coldness which had conspired at its end.

'For God's sake, David, that was nearly thirty years ago! You were angling for a place on the first XV. I was travelling half-fare on buses!'

'And Mam was bringing us up on her own while he swanned around foreign ports impressing cheap women with his uniform.'

'Mam.' Well, he'd brought her up. 'OK, David, I'm going to tell you something about our mother – whom I loved at least as much as you did, but whom I knew rather better. You're angry because Da was unfaithful to her? She was unfaithful to him all their married life, and she married him fully intending to be. Her only real love was this house. It was to be her dowry, so she needed a husband. She wanted someone to pass it on to, so she needed children – '

I could have been really cruel and told him that what she wanted was a daughter, to fashion in her own image and leave at the last in her own house, her subtle tenacious immortality, but even when his lack of understanding drove me to harsh words I never wanted to hurt him.

'You think it's a coincidence she married a sailor, who would leave her alone in her house with her children for most of the year? She didn't care what he fathered on who, David, as long he fathered you and me on her, and didn't get the idea that was a right rather than a duty.'

David stared at me, not too drunk to comprehend, and in the depths of his blue eyes he was appalled. In not much more than a whisper he said, 'She told you this?'

'No. But she knew I knew.' Even before but more so after David's marriage, when we were two women sharing a somewhat isolated lifestyle on the side of a Welsh hill, we were intimately – almost incestuously – close. I was more than just her daughter. I was the next tenant of her house.

We didn't talk any more that night. I called Jan to say David was staying over, making some excuse that would reassure her without inviting the kind of cross-examination I couldn't take right now even from a sister-in-law and friend; and when I went back into the living-room my brother was asleep, curled round his empty glass in a corner of the settee, his breathing sonorous. I eased his shoes off and his legs up on to the settee, and threw a quilt over him and went back to bed. My dreams were confused, fragmentary, and when I woke it was morning and David had gone.

2

I called school to say I wouldn't be in. They sounded startled – as well they might, in the twelve years I had been there I had missed only one day, when a small winter landslide carried my road away – and then curious, but I made no attempt to explain. I had covered for enough absent colleagues in twelve years – dear God, I had even taken the rugby squad – to expect some of them to cover for me now. Even the veiled threat that the only free periods in the day belonged to Dr Daniel Roberts, DD, whose idea of history was the military application of shofars in the prosecution of a siege, failed to deter me. I could always get my own back, next time he was away at a synod or something, by telling his divinity students that Ahab was a just ruler, Jezebel a liberal queen, and the Book of Kings a party political broadcast on behalf of Solomon written in support of his rather tenuous claim to the throne of Israel. I can't understand people who find history dull!

Then I phoned Mr Arkwright's office to tell him when to expect me. His secretary wasn't sure he would be free. I told her I could wait. She decided he would probably be free after all.

The solicitor was not only free when I arrived but waiting for me, and he ushered me courteously into his small office where cups and a big silver pot were laid out on his desk. At least he wasn't expecting to deal with me in three minutes flat.

'Miss Meredith, come and sit down.' He pronounced it the English way, which made me smile: he would certainly have been corrected, so the error had been propagated deliberately, to annoy my father. My father had a way of inviting such gestures, as others invite compliments or confidences. When I was ordering his tombstone I had to fight the urge to inscribe: 'Beneath this sod lies another one.'

The Arkwrights had been in the family solicitor business since Victorian times, which was clearly when their corporate image was created. Our Mr Arkwright still wore dark, square-cut suits virtually indistinguishable from his grandfather's, and the same square-cut greying beard with just enough room for a smile before it met his full moustache. Physically, too, he seemed designed more for Dickens than the space programme: of middle height and more than middle girth, with rosy cherubic cheeks, large soft pink hands and eyes like twinkling grey diamonds. I couldn't imagine how David Copperfield got by without him.

His voice came from the same place: deep and warm and infinitely reassuring, not at all the sort of voice you'd expect to pronounce your name wrong deliberately. 'How's your brother? I'm afraid what I had to tell him yesterday came as rather a shock.'

'You find that surprising?'

'Hardly surprising. But – '

'Just because David is built like Cader Idris doesn't mean he's impervious to hurt. That was quite a bombshell you dropped.'

'Yes, of course.' He poured the coffee. It turned out, predictably, to be tea. 'You too, I'm sure, found the news disturbing.'

I tried not to smile. He was astute as well, our Mr

Arkwright. 'In our family,' I said, 'the men have all the height, breadth and physical strength. The women have a different kind of toughness.'

He nodded in unexpectedly candid agreement. I had to keep reminding myself that he was not a near stranger but a man who had known more about my family than I had for probably longer than I had been alive. 'That's what your father said. It's a matter of considerable regret to me that I never met your mother.'

'She was the noblest Meredith of us all,' I said, not without irony, giving the name its Welsh pronunciation in gentle but overt reproof. 'Mr Arkwright, it wasn't the members of my family that I've known since childhood that I came here to discuss.'

His initial response was that, as of twelve hours ago, I knew as much as he did. He had never met my father's younger son, after all; his role had been solely in the allocation of monies in accordance with the old man's instructions. A standing order at his bank could have done much the same job; and learned as much about the boy, his hopes and his fears and the things that made him feel good.

But when at my request he pulled the file, the old records set Mr Arkwright to remembering. Not much, my father had never confided in him, only used his professional services, but fragments of a real life scattered like pressed flowers through the pages of his heavy ledgers.

She had been just nineteen, Señorita Baez – her name, Margarita, was mentioned only once in all those papers – the only child of a prosperous middle-class family who doubtless had other plans for her than bearing a half-breed lovechild. They were introduced by her father, who had known the old man for some years, knew he was married and a father, and thought nothing untoward could come of entertaining the foreign captain at his home one empty Sunday between voyages.

There was no clue as to what had happened: love, infatuation, mere opportunism. It ended when my father took his ship back to sea. There were no clues as to how she felt, as a child of her race and breeding facing an illegitimate pregnancy in the early sixties, except that she had somehow managed to keep her condition a secret until the eighth month when she haemorrhaged, was rushed into hospital and delivered of a scrap of premature humanity that wasn't expected to last the day. A priest was hurried in to christen it Cristóbal. The hospital bill, enclosed with a brief and bitter letter from Señor Baez, was the first notice my father had that his short liaison with the pilot's daughter had borne fruit.

His response was entirely in character. He challenged not the issue of paternity, nor even that of jurisdiction, but the size of the bill. He enquired if it was normal practice in Mexico for hospital confinements to last fifteen days.

Though the pilot now corresponded through his own lawyer, the note of outrage was unmistakable. In Mexico as elsewhere, he wrote, complications could arise, particularly where a first pregnancy had occurred against a background of difficult circumstances; nor was Señorita Baez a peasant girl who might be expected to return to her work in the tobacco fields a few hours after completing her labours on the puerperal bed.

When it became clear that the child was not going to do the convenient thing and die, arrangements for his future had to be made. Baez's lawyer conveyed the information that his client did not propose to accept his daughter's bastard into his home. Either my father would take the boy or, at his expense, a couple would be found to foster him.

I knew how he had chosen. I wondered how long he had deliberated: if he had agonised over the decision, or dashed off a cheque in the next post.

Mr Arkwright remembered something of the time. 'It wasn't easy for him, Miss Meredith. I think he'd have liked to take the child. He had me enquire into the legal procedure. But a couple of days later he called me and said to forget about it and send the money instead. It was then that he set up the fund. He made certain investments over to it so that he wouldn't have to write cheques. I administered it for him. He never asked how the boy was doing, and I understood that I was not to volunteer information. I broke that unspoken injunction only once – well, up till now, that is.'

'What happened?'

When Cristóbal was fifteen the woman who raised him – alone to all intents and purposes, having been widowed ten years before – walked in front of a bicycle while shopping for groceries, fell awkwardly and broke her hip. Her married daughter took her in to care for her, but lacked the room in her small rented apartment for a teenage foster-brother as well. She tried to keep her eye on him, but one day when she went round with food and laundry she found him gone, headed north to make his fortune in the land of opportunity.

For almost six months Mr Arkwright heard nothing more. Señora Delgado's daughter had written explaining that since Cristóbal was no longer under her roof her mother would not be accepting further payments for his keep, and asking to be informed if Mr Arkwright heard from him, if only to say that he was safe.

'And then one day in the post, in a fancy envelope under a fancy stamp, I got this letter from a hospital in Fort Worth, saying they understood I administered funds for one Cristóbal Baez and would I please send them two thousand dollars on account for his treatment for a ruptured kidney and sundry other injuries … '

When people finish a sentence their voices drop. Mr Arkwright's rose on the last syllable: he hadn't finished what he had intended to say, rather he had thought better of it.

I said, 'Go on.' He looked uncertain. 'Was he robbing a bank? Was he beaten up trying to mug a seventy-year-old ju-jitsu expert? Was he selling his body for the price of beer and enchiladas?'

Mr Arkwright said, 'Yes.'

Winter in Texas had been colder, hungrier and perhaps more lonely than he had been ready for. He tried to get work but jobs were hard to come by and harder to keep for a half-breed teenager in a country that wasn't his, with no papers, no skills, not even much English. For a time he starved. Finally someone offered him work he could do, where Border Patrol wouldn't ask for his papers and Highway Patrol wouldn't want to see his driving licence, and he took it.

And sometime after that a dissatisfied customer laid into him with his fists and his boots and probably pieces of furniture, and dumped him on the freeway from a moving car.

'You sent the money?' I asked.

'Indeed. The trust's investments had done very well, there was a good surplus in the fund, but anyway your father said I was to send what was necessary, he'd find the difference if the fund ran dry. He wanted to go there, too, to see the boy.'

The heart within me gave a sudden unexpected leap. Finally I had a point of contact with my half-brother. I remembered that week eleven years ago when my father, already an old man, phoned from the airport – I could hear the planes muffled in the background – to say he would be away for maybe a fortnight and he'd let me know when to come and pick him up.

I was astounded. He hadn't been away for a night since he had retired and come home. He didn't do anything on impulse, not even getting a haircut. When I found my voice I tried to argue, but he bade me a curt farewell and put the phone down. I didn't even know which airport he had called from.

It was Birmingham, and three hours later a Birmingham hospital phoned me to say they had admitted my father to their coronary unit after he was taken ill while arguing with the boarding-staff about the proportion of smoking to non-smoking seats on a 747.

His life was never in any danger, but they kept him for a couple of weeks before sending him home with a list of instructions touching on virtually every aspect of his life – his diet, alcohol intake, smoking (a sin only marginally the right side of child molestation as far as doctors are concerned), exercise, sleeping habits and permitted states of mind. Worry in particular was strictly proscribed: they spelt out unambiguously the likely consequences, so that anyone who wasn't worried before was sure as hell worried afterwards.

The night it happened I drove over to Birmingham, only to find him sedated insensible by the time I arrived. They said he had been in a state of acute anxiety. Three more times I made the journey, to sit with him and talk and make plans for when he got home, but I never got a coherent account of why he had been arguing with airline staff about his seat on a transatlantic flight. After the first time I asked he simply ignored any attempt to broach the subject.

The first time, though, when he was still pretty sick and almost delirious, I got a kind of answer, although I had never until now understood it. He had said, 'I tried to go. Remember that – I tried to go.' He could not or would not tell me where, or why.

And now I knew. 'Obviously the boy recovered.'

'Oh yes,' said Mr Arkwright. 'Not overnight, you understand, or indeed completely – the hospital told me he'd be stuck with a suspect kidney for the rest of his life. But he was pretty much all right when he left there.' He frowned, the features grouping together within the frame of his hair and beard. 'They let me down there, the hospital. Which in view of all the money I was sending them was a little cheeky. That's colonials for you.'

I smiled. Whatever else had come of this conversation,

whatever answers it had provided and whatever new
questions it had raised, I had learned one thing – that my
family solicitor was not only a clever man and a humorous
man but an ally. I trusted him.

And I think he was a caring man too. My father's
business had required of him a degree of detachment, and
there is anyway a limit to the amount of feeling you can put
into writing a cheque. But even if he had not intended to,
he had ended up caring for my little brother, and for that I
was grateful.

'They were supposed to call me when he was due for
release. I planned to go out there, sign him out and make
some arrangements for his future – in the States, in
Mexico, find him a job or a school or *something*: something
that would keep him off the streets. Oh, I don't know what
I expected to achieve, but I meant to have a damn good
try. Apart from anything else it seemed important to me
that he should know there were people who cared about
him, who could help if the going got tough.

'Well, Murphy's Law intervened. Instead of telephoning
the hospital wrote to say Cristóbal was being discharged.
By the time I got the letter he had been out for three days
and I couldn't find him. I even called in the Fort Worth
police – he was an illegal immigrant, a juvenile and already
implicated in vice in the city: I thought at least behind bars
he'd be safe enough while we worked out what to do about
him. But when they went to the address he had given the
hospital, there was nothing there – it was a hole in the
ground where a derelict building had fallen in. He was
gone, back into the underground. The police reckoned
their only real chance of finding him again was if
somebody smashed his other kidney.'

We sat for a time in silence. It was, after all, more or less
what had happened. Mr Arkwright replenished our cups.

'You never heard from him again?' That wasn't quite
what David had said. I struggled to remember.

'No, he reappeared about four years later, in prison in

Monterrey. Señora Delgado's daughter wrote to me to say he was awaiting trial on charges of robbing an antique dealer and she was going to see him. Then she wrote again, begging me to send him money. Apparently Mexican jails aren't the most comfortable but it is possible to buy a certain amount of privilege. In the absence of such protection just about everybody in the place was beating up on him. She was convinced he would be dead before he could be tried.

'I talked to your father about it. The hospital bills had made a big hole in the trust fund but there was still a respectable figure left. He instructed me to make it over to Señora Delgado, for use in Cristóbal's interests as she saw them, on the clear understanding that there was no more to come. In another month or so he'd turn twenty-one, he had picked the life he wanted to lead, he must now bear the consequences of it.

'Again, I offered to go out there, see what I could do for him. Your father pointed out that with the money he could buy a local lawyer familiar with defending young thugs in Mexican courts. He was right, of course, but I can't help wishing I had gone anyway. I had never worried about displeasing your father before, I don't know why I picked such a hell of a time to start.'

'Was he convicted?'

'It never came to trial. Apparently he used the money with some skill, because soon afterwards all sorts of technical flaws in the case against him were discovered and the charges were withdrawn. And that really was the last I heard of him, until yesterday.'

There was one thing more in the file – deep in, buried among those first angry letters. Where it had come from we couldn't imagine: certainly not Cristóbal's grandfather, or his lawyer. We sat quietly together, Mr Arkwright and I, sharing a sorrow and looking at this last piece of evidence: a small black and white photograph of a very young, very poised, really very beautiful Mexican girl. It was, of course, Señorita Baez – Cristóbal's mother, my father's mistress.

And there was one thing more on my mind. 'After the child was born, when my father was toying with the idea of taking him – do you think he asked my mother?'

He considered for a moment, assessing me with his grey diamond eyes. 'You want my honest opinion?' I nodded. 'Then yes, I think he did.'

I thought so too. And she had said no.

3

I didn't actually decide.I was going to America until after I had begun my interview with the headmaster: about the time he started lecturing me (very politely, with hardly a glimpse of the mailed fist within the academic velvet glove) about my responsibilities – to him, to the school and to my class, few of whom could distinguish between the Black Prince and the Black Death and all of whom preferred 'The Black Adder'.

Even then he just might have avoided the problems of replacing a teacher midway through the winter had he not mistaken my silence for consent and appealed, with a paternalistic smile that was meant to make me feel warm and secure, to my sense of family honour.

'After all,' he said, smiling, 'it's a great pleasure for us to have Marged Gruffydd's daughter teaching at our school. Your mother is still remembered with great fondness and respect by those of us who were privileged to know her. And of course, your brother was one of our most memorable captains of rugby.'

'And my other brother,' I said, very calmly, although he must have heard the anger in my voice, 'died ten days ago, crossing illegally into the United States in the back of a refrigerated lorry, and I intend to know why. Mr Price, I didn't come in here to apologise for being away yesterday. I came to advise you that, starting tomorrow, I shall be away for some weeks.

'Our little talk just now has however persuaded me that would be a mistake. You'll have my resignation by close of play today. I'm sorry I can't give you the proper notice. I'm going to London tomorrow and flying out as soon as the arrangements are made.

'As for my mother, I'm not altogether sure she deserved your admiration. But whatever else she did, I shall always be grateful to her for providing me with the financial independence which makes it possible for me to indicate what you may do with your responsibilities, your respect and indeed your rugby.'

I left him open-mouthed – in Wales you *never* slang rugby – and even the knowledge that notoriety would attend me all the rest of my days in that small, inward-looking community because of what I had just done could not detract much from the pleasure of it.

David, when I told him what I was doing, what I had done, reacted with characteristic enthusiasm. '*Why*, in God's name?' he demanded. 'Hell fire, you know you'll never get another job? Not here you won't. You told him *what*? Oh, dammo!'

He thought I had burnt my boats on the spur of the moment, piqued by Mr Price's attitude, and he was right. He thought when I calmed down a little I would regret it, and in that he was wrong.

It wasn't wholly, or perhaps even mainly, to do with Cristóbal. Yes, I felt guilty about him, and angry, and more resentful than I can say that I had had a half-brother who no one had thought to mention until he was dead. I felt a craving need to discover him and explore him, and since he was now stone cold on a slab that was going to be difficult, but there was an ache in me that would haunt me to my own grave if I didn't at least try. If I couldn't know Cristóbal, I could at least see the places he had come from, learn something of the pressures which had driven him; come to terms if I could, by being there, with the fact that someone had left my brother to die in the back of a sealed truck because it was more convenient than letting him out. I felt I owed him that much. Our family's money, which might have prevented his death and didn't, could at least buy this last personal tribute, which would make me feel better if it did nothing for him. That was the part that was to do with Cristóbal.

The part that wasn't went back a long way. I had lived here, apart from my university years, all my life. I had taken the job at my local school because it enabled me to go on living here, in my mother's house. I had had opportunities to advance my career and, for the same reason, had done nothing about them. My entire life had become not so much a rut as a trench, plush-lined but still infinitely limiting in its comfortable restrictions.

There was nothing new in this, of course, not even the awareness. It was what I had wanted and I had been prepared to pay the price. Only somewhere along the line the price had got too high. There were places I should have been, people I should have met, too many things I should have done and hadn't. The realisation had been growing in me, unacknowledged, almost but not quite unnoticed, that I was living the life of an old lady, and when I was an old lady for real I would look back with regret for all the chances I hadn't taken.

And Cristóbal was a catalyst there too, because he had lived by taking chances and finally taking one chance too many had killed him. I wasn't stupid, I had no wish to share that much uncertainty, but it put into unflattering perspective my reluctance to gamble on the milkman remembering to cancel my order and the neighbours remembering to feed my dogs.

'David,' I said at last, 'I'm going to his funeral. That's all. I'm going to pay my respects because someone from his family ought to be there.'

'The funeral is probably over now.'

I breathed heavily at him. 'If I'm the only mourner, we'll

damn well have the funeral when I get there – even if we have to dig him up to do it.'

I put the days in London to good use. I called first at Grosvenor Square to apply for my visa and took the opportunity, when the attache asked the purpose of my visit, to fix him with a glittering Ancient Mariner eye and tell him my tale, only slightly abridged from the original epic version.

He was a decent man, anxious to help if he could, though I could see behind his gaze to where he wondered what I hoped to achieve by going there. I wasn't surprised he didn't understand; if he had, I'd have asked him to explain it to me.

He promised to make a few enquiries for me and had me go back the following afternoon. This time I left with my visa, with a letter on embassy notepaper asking that I be given all reasonable assistance by the US authorities, and a handful of names and phone numbers where I might make useful contacts.

My second call was to the British Museum. It was twelve months since I had been there last, several years since I had spent any real time there. I wasn't sure how many people I would still know. But I needn't have worried: nothing changes that quickly in a museum.

I spent most of the day there, concentrating on the meso-American exhibits but gradually being tempted into lengthy asides among the wider pre-Columbian collection: the mummies, the flutes, the toys mounted on wheels for children whose parents never learned to apply the principle to lightening their own labours, the knotted strings that were the only information technology available to a civil service running a society three thousand mountainous miles long. (I'm a bit of an Inca fan: it seems to me that a people who could get useful work out of something as basically contrary as the llama deserved a great deal better than Francisco Pizarro.) I admired the use of gold in jewellery and statuary, and the reed boats, and the carved stones. Then I went back to my hotel, wondering whether it was good news or bad that I had picked up among the stelae.

I finally decided it was good news, that there was a major excavation going on in Yucatan led by a man I had known at and since university, where I would be welcomed (perhaps not effusively) as a professional and which would give me a valid reason for visiting Mexico. But satisfaction was laced with just a small regret that the archaeologist in question, the man I had known for twenty years and it didn't seem a day too short, was Richard Balfour, a person whom as he grew older and cleverer even his mother must have found it increasingly difficult to like.

It occurred to me only later to wonder why I had felt the need to research an alibi before entering a friendly country where I had legitimate interests and no enemies. I hadn't known, before, that I had inherited – along with my mother's house and my father's temper – the gift of second sight.

There may be better places in the world to get used to driving a hired car on the wrong side of the road – the Gobi Desert springs to mind – but the highway which took me across the Edwards Plateau, across the River Pecos and finally across the El Paso railway track and into the border lands was a pretty good choice. It wasn't that there was no traffic – there was, particularly in the early part of the journey – more that it was nicely spaced out, you could see it coming often for miles, and most of it stuck religiously to the speed limit. I probably broke it more than anybody: once I was at ease with the big car it took a positive effort to tie it down on that wide open road.

Not only the road was wide open. Mountains loomed in the distance beyond the Pecos, but I knew from my map it would take me hours to reach them. Otherwise the horizon was endlessly broad, and the pale sky above it the biggest thing I had ever seen.

What surprised me most, though, was the snow. This was Texas, setting for a thousand films, and in every one of them if the Indians didn't get you the desert sun did. Historically, this land was so hot and so arid that stealing a man's horse was the same as murdering him and was treated as such. But this desert was high, maybe three thousand feet above sea level, and even in daylight host to a cramping cold, and some little pocket of moisture must have been whipped up off the Gulf of Mexico and dragged up here to fall as snow. It lay in long drifts pricked through by dead dry scrub, and in wind-driven heaps behind rocks and in the folds of the land. It was a moonscape bathed in earthshine, a place where it seemed nothing could live. I checked the map again. Somewhere between here and those mountains my brother and his companions had been shut in a tin box and left to die.

I stopped the car and got out, to see what that felt like. The desert washed against both edges of the tarmac, breaking in a foam of hardcore. The hardcore was rimed with frost and the sandy soil with a sugaring of crisp, brittle snowflakes that crushed to nothing under my boots. The wind blew the white particles away, glittering like glass dust as they flew.

The wind was like the sky: big beyond all normal comprehension of scale, powerful beyond measure. It wasn't blowing at any great speed, whipping the blood into my cheeks and the breath from my mouth: I was just profoundly aware of the absolute enormity of it, a wind measured not in knots but by the thousand square miles. It was like a vast army on the march – slow and steady now, but overwhelming in its potential for destruction. When this wind really blew, all the way from the Rockies maybe with nothing in between to break its strength, it would be the biggest thing in all that huge landscape. And the coldest. Even now, with the pale sun high in the pale sky, blue like the hearts of icebergs, its chill fingers stroked across my face like meltwater and groped inside my heavy coat, searching my body, less like a lover than a policeman. The desert was no less a killer in winter than under the hottest of summer suns.

At first, probably, when they realised they had been abandoned, the men in the trailer would, in the spirit of being grateful for small mercies, have expressed relief that at least they hadn't the hard coppery sun of the midyear beating down on them. They would imagine the metal panels heating up to roasting point, to where they would sear the skin, and they would huddle into their winter coats with some gratitude and wait for rescue, believing they had maybe a few days before the lack of water would become critical. They would expect to be found before that.

But their air supply was also finite, and there were seven of them breathing it; and even if there had been air, the cold would have killed them long before the thirst. The metal would have grown cold enough to burn, cold enough that unprotected skin would freeze to it and tear before it could be pulled away. In his last minutes of life, after the oxygen in the truck had been breathed and rebreathed until there wasn't enough left to feed muscles or will, my brother's sapped and cooling body would have slumped against the bitter steel and he would have felt the skin of his hands and his face cleave to it, freezing him like a carcase in a coldroom even before death intervened.

I got back in the car and turned up the heater, and drove on to Sarajevo.

Anyone who has crossed a land border anywhere has been to Sarajevo. It is hardly so much a place as a state of mind. Sarajevo was created to service the border in the same way as transport cafes were created to service the articulated lorry, and shared the same sort of reality. It was a place of some size but no dimension, flat, constructed of numerous identically square elements, all the same colour – the colour of sand. It might have been a film-set, six months after the end of filming when the wind and the rain have had time to strip away the gloss. It was an MGM ghost-town, and I found myself looking not so much for sagebush bowling in the gutters by the boardwalks as for tangles of discarded rushes bearing away their moments of cinematic history on the cold dry wind.

The border ran through the centre of town. It wasn't a big deal of a border, like Checkpoint Charlie in Berlin. It ran across the main street, apparently delineated by a barber's shop to the north and a hardware store to the south. There were customs posts on both the US and the Mexican sides, but there seemed to be some quite casual coming and going too. Cars travelling in either direction were stopped and those entering the US were searched, sometimes quite thoroughly. Commercial traffic was subjected to rigorous scrutiny, but people on foot were seldom challenged. Watching, I got the impression that the town, while split politically between two nations, acted socially and geographically as one entity. Everybody bought their vegetables in Mexico; everybody got their electricals repaired at Ed Quiery's in Texas. The barber's had two doors but only one chair. I wondered who he paid his taxes to.

Like border towns everywhere, Sarajevo was about half made up of government offices: customs offices and immigration offices, and the offices of the US Border Patrol and police. The other half was businesses that could hardly have survived a sudden treaty adopting Mexico as the 51st state. There were importers and exporters, and transporters and transport cafes, and petrol stations and cheap souvenir shops, and bad expensive ethnic restaurants for the tourists and good cheap chili kitchens for the locals who knew better. There was even a livery stable, within sight of the frontier post, advertising saddle treks into the Heartland of Old Mexico – an hour's hike around five miles of Mexican dust indistinguishable from the Texan dust I had driven in through.

And for those who knew how to look, which as yet I did not, there would be the other border businesses: the purveyors of fake papers, the suppliers of illicit labour, the dealers in Mexican brown and cocaine, the agents for the acquisition by wealthy, discreet collectors of unlicensed archaeological artifacts.

And somewhere, in this town or the next, or another I would somehow find, a man who made his living by importing illegal aliens and dealt with the threat the law occasionally posed by destroying the evidence. It had come to me, somewhere on the drive through that bitter desolation, what I had come here for. I had come to find my brother's past, his family, his hopes or fears that had driven him to his death among the frozen rocks of a winter plain; and I had also come to find his murderer.

Joshua Cade was a lucky strike. The man at Grosvenor Square who gave me his name had done his homework. He was a young man – well, younger than me, mid-thirties perhaps – but he wasn't marking time waiting for something more prestigious than Sarajevo to come along. He had gone into Border Patrol because it interested him, it was what he wanted to do, and he had learnt his subject, in theory and in practice, inside out and back to front.

He knew who I was. He had been warned to expect me. He knew about Cristóbal's death. He also knew the names of the six other Mexicans who died in the truck, and where each of them had come from and the sort of life he was trying to escape.

'And my brother: what was he escaping from?'

Cade had a nice face – intelligent, sensitive, honest. The brown eyes were sympathetic, not patronising. 'Do you know he was in prison?'

'That was six years ago.'

'That's the last record either government has of him. His family, such as it was – ' He stopped and coloured darkly under the wind-tan. 'I'm sorry, I mean the woman who raised him and her daughter – they say they've seen him maybe four or five times since then. Each time he arrived without warning, stayed overnight and left in the morning. The daughter, Pilar, saw him last – about nine months ago. She said he seemed OK. He left some money with her, for her mother. About five hundred dollars' worth; he'd done the same a few times before. So he wasn't broke, but he probably wasn't robbing any banks either.'

I thought about it. 'If he'd had a job – a legal job – wouldn't there have been some record of that?'

'Probably.'

'So maybe he was robbing small banks.'

He smiled at that. He had a nice smile, too. 'A lot of people, both sides of this border, make money in ways that wouldn't seem strictly legal back in England, Miss Meredith. They don't seem strictly legal in Washington either, so we get the job of stopping as much as we can. But it doesn't make all of them bad people. When we found your brother, he wasn't carrying a gun and he wasn't carrying drugs, and he had only enough money to keep him for a couple of weeks while he found work. He was as much a victim of the border as the other six.'

We sat drinking his coffee. It was good not feeling I had to say something or leave. At length I said, with perhaps more feeling than I had intended, 'I don't even know what he looked like.'

Cade looked at me with a depth of thinking in his eyes. Then he said, 'He was a nice looking kid. Mixed blood; so which of us round here hasn't?' The tan was not entirely due to wind and sun, then. 'A bit smaller than me – shorter, thinner – maybe he hadn't been eating too well. Or maybe he just had small bones, like you. He had the same green eyes.'

Unexpectedly, that felt like a hand clutching my heart. 'You saw him?'

'Miss Meredith, I found him. It was some way from here but still our territory. You didn't know that?'

'No.' I couldn't see why it mattered. But it clearly did,

because there were tears behind my eyes and in my voice, and it was only the shame of crying for one man I didn't know in front of another that kept me from breaking down.

Cade saw my distress. 'I'm sorry, I – ' His voice was low and gentle, and in it there was something else that I sensed rather than heard and anyway did not understand: something almost like remorse.

He recovered quicker than I did. 'Listen, are you ready to eat? There are some rubbish diners in this town, but there are good ones too. We'll go to Flanaghan's.'

'An Irish restaurant?'

'Jésus Flanaghan's,' he grinned. 'I told you, we've mostly got mixed blood round here. Where are you staying, do you want to change first?'

'Is it posh?' He didn't understand. 'Classy?'

'You really are a stranger, aren't you?'

We walked. It was two blocks down and over the border; we crossed without ceremony. It was as near nothing as a border could be, far too little a thing for a man to die attempting. I don't know what I had expected – not the Berlin wall, certainly, with machine-guns, watch towers, minefields and Dobermanns, but something more than a couple of amiable young men looking at whatever was presented to them more from politeness than any obvious desire to separate sheep and goats. A shade bitterly, because I felt they should be taking more care of something my brother had died trying to steal, I remarked as much to Cade.

'Don't underestimate them,' he said. 'They know this town, this land. They know everybody who lives here, everybody who works here, everybody who visits four times a year to stock up on goods and gossip. They probably know most of the population for thirty miles around. They know those people, like me, they don't have to give a second glance; and they know those, like him' – I hadn't noticed and Cade didn't seem to have looked back but the guards had stopped a brown car and were politely but firmly escorting the American driver to the rear – 'they don't pass without checking down to the axles; and they know a few faces they don't challenge at the border, they call my people and we meet them on the road with sufficient manpower and weaponry to be sure of holding them, and no bystanders to get hurt.

'And most everybody else, they look close enough to know if they're muling – carrying drugs, smuggling illegals, some other contraband – and they don't make too many mistakes.'

'Do you get much violence?'

He shook his head. He had rather long, straight dark hair that he kept out of his eyes by small, regular, unconscious flicks of his head, like a horse. He looked more Indian than Mexican. 'Not much. Hardly ever from the illegals, and hardly ever in town. You have to remember, Miss Meredith, this border's fourteen hundred miles long. There are places it's hard to know just where it is. We can regulate the heavy traffic, most of the cars, pretty well all the tourists, because they use the roads and we've got posts on them. But you get off the roads – on foot, on horseback, with four-wheel drive – and let's be honest here, you've got a good chance of getting through. Last year we caught two million illegals. We reckon we missed as many again.'

'I wish you'd caught my brother.'

'So do I.' Again that hunted, haunted sound in his voice. 'So do I.'

4

Jésus Flanaghan did a nice line in things I was rather pleased to discover I could both recognise and pronounce, and no stew at all. It was strange, the way the names and the tastes slipped suddenly into focus. None of them, of course, was entirely alien to me – I had eaten Mexican, in Cardiff; I had learnt Spanish in school. Since I was old enough to know why my father never made prize-givings, I had known about this land, and read and learnt what I could about it – almost as an antidote to that faint, pervasive sense of loss. If I couldn't have my father – I was young enough, then, to forget in between visits how traumatic those visits could be – I could at least share in the things that kept him away. I knew a lot about ships, too, and once beat up one Aled Evans who claimed the wide-bodied jet would make commercial shipping redundant.

But coming here, eating albondigas with Joshua Cade, was different. The Mexico I knew about was bigger, older, grander, more important – it was Mexico City, the old Aztec capital of Tenochtitlan; it was Veracruz, dating back to the bloody Spanyard of 1519; it was the temples of Teotihuacan and Chichen Itza, the Olmec heads, the Maya stelae; it was Quetzalcoatl, the feathered serpent, and Chac, guardian of the rainclouds.

Flanaghan's meatballs were not more real than those things but they were more immediate. It was the difference between knowing a country from books and knowing her by her smell. At that moment Mexico was full of people who knew less about her than I did, but none of them would have been taken aback, however momentarily, by the discovery that real Mexican waiters wear aprons, like any other waiters, and save their ponchos for going out in the rain. I felt a fraud, and thanked God that Cade had never heard me holding forth on the subject of this land, its history and its people. Apart from facts, I knew next to nothing.

And about my brother's death, not even the facts. 'So what went wrong?' I asked. 'If it's so easy that two million people manage it every year, why did seven others die in the back of that truck – after they'd already crossed the border, for God's sake? Where's the sense in that?'

Cade didn't answer at once. Then he said, 'The people coming north are trying to get away from poverty, from living and dying on the subsistence line. Some of them are so poor they have nowhere to live – literally nowhere, only the hills. It costs too much for them to educate their children, and the kids get sick a lot. They eat beans, nothing else. For four or five months after the tobacco crop is finished in June, there's no work, not even at four dollars a day, so they get together all the money they can – sometimes they get help from relatives who wish they'd tried when they were younger – and invest it, gamble it if you like, on the chance of making a new life in the US.

'Half of them make it. They work hard – any hotel will tell you undocumented workers do twice as much as legal ones – and keep their heads down and don't give anybody any trouble. They're exploited like hell, and they know it – there are businesses in all the southern states that couldn't survive without Mexican illegals, so they threaten to send them back if they won't co-operate.

'Still, their life in the north is a whole lot better than what most of them have left, so they stay – as long as they can, as long as they can avoid the raids. If they get picked up we push them through the revolving door – illegal entry is a criminal offence, but it's not worth anybody's while prosecuting – and they start saving up to come back. If they don't get picked up they save to bring their sisters and their sons north too. These aren't bad people; they're desperate people doing the best they can with the hand they have, and if I wasn't paid to keep them out I'd be more than half inclined to help them get in.

'But the people who bring them are something else. They do it for the money, nothing else, and they don't take any risks they don't have to. A lot of them mule drugs at the same time, some of them smuggle out unlicensed artifacts. But there's money enough in wetbacks if you want to specialise – the rate varies but the average is currently around three hundred dollars a head, plus any kickback you can arrange for supplying cheap labour. The expenses are low – transport, wages, pay-offs – both sides of the border. About half of it is clear profit. Three hundred dollars is about three months' wages in Mexico, if you can get the work.'

He hadn't mentioned my brother once, but he'd told me probably all there was to know about the kind of life he had. It began to make understanding possible. I could see how Cristóbal had come to where he died; and more and more I wanted those who killed him.

Something he had said echoed. 'Do you get much corruption on your side?' I was not so much surprised that it happened as that he admitted it.

He smiled, a shade tightly. 'It happens. I've known people who took the money and got caught. I've probably known others who took it and didn't, and I've known some who were offered it and put the bastards in jail.'

'And you?'

'I was never offered it.'

'You'd have put the bastards in jail?'

'Oh yes,' he said with conviction.

'You don't have to wonder?'

'No. I don't do this job because I enjoy rounding up illegals. I do it for the pleasure – '

' – Of putting the bastards in jail,' I finished.

We both smiled but he was absolutely serious and I believed him. He went on. 'This isn't the first time. It's new to you and personal, but I have found dead Mexicans before, on my roads and in my hills and in my river, and while some of them died taking the risks of the crossing, some were disposed of because they came to threaten the smooth running of a profitable operation – they asked the wrong questions, saw the wrong people, or maybe they got sick, or maybe they got demanding. A good wet-back's supposed just to pay his three hundred dollars then go where he's sent and do what he's told, and take any abuse and any exploitation that involves without complaint. And dear God, most of them take it; but when they take it on my territory, that makes it personal to me.'

He felt me staring at him and the angry torrent of words came to an end, but mostly because he had finished what he wanted to say. He wasn't embarrassed by the strength of his feelings. They were why he was here, in this dusty, windy, back-of-beyond little border town, fighting graft and complacency and a central administration that neither understood the problem nor paid more than lip-service towards its solution, and through all that measuring success in terms of a fifty percent failure rate. It was a hell of a job, an almost impossible job: he had to care either too much or not at all.

'You think that's what Cristóbal did – complain?'

Across his eyes, so open with anger, flitted again that strange shadow of reticence. 'Maybe.' He gave an awkward little shrug that raised one shoulder more than the other. 'There were seven men in that truck. It may have been nothing to do with your brother. Maybe it was nothing to do with any of them – the driver may have thought we were on his tail.'

'But you weren't.'

'No.'

'Or you'd have got to them before they died.'

'I'm sorry,' he said with sudden intensity. 'I'm sorry we couldn't save him. We tried. We found them: it was too late. I'm sorry. But I can't change it for you.'

I realised I was being unfair, obscurely blaming him for what had happened. He didn't need me to tell him that if he had done differently that day, patrolled earlier or later, taken this track instead of that one, seven dead men would still be alive. It was a burden he'd carry the rest of his life. I hoped he would have the strength to know that he wasn't responsible for other men's crimes or other men's luck. He had neither killed my brother nor created the situation in which he had been killed. He had failed, through no fault

of his own and possibly quite narrowly, to save those seven
lives. If things had turned out differently he'd have been
hailed as a hero, but that would have been luck too. It's as
much as a man can carry to be responsible for his actions:
his luck, good or bad, must rest in other realms.

I laid my hand on his forearm, felt through his sleeve
the long muscles relax as his fist unclenched. 'No, I'm
sorry. Thank you for finding him. Thank you for trying.'

As we walked back over the border, meriting another of
those casual, astute looks from the guards – this time one
of them asked me to state my citizenship and if I had
bought anything, and because Cade was with me I resisted
the temptation to tell them I was a Cuban revolutionary
smuggling Havana cigars – I said what I had been working
myself up to say. 'Joshua, where is he buried?'

He didn't break his stride, but he didn't exactly answer
either. 'Buried?'

Cristóbal had been dead now for over a fortnight. This
was a hot land – not right now, but they'd be used to
making arrangements promptly. Since he was at least
nominally a Catholic I presumed they would not have
cremated him. 'I want to see his grave.'

We went back to his office. It was quieter now evening
was coming on, pale lamps blooming in the streets, haloed
by the frost hanging in the air, but there was still activity
and purpose about the place. A patrol went out as we came
in, in a dusty two-tone jeep that offered only cloth-top
protection against the gathering cold. Both men were
armed.

'To be honest, Annie,' said Cade – I wouldn't ask anyone
outside Wales to tackle Angharad – 'I don't know where he
is. They took the bodies to Leyton, to the hospital there.
They'd be released to any family that came forward, but I
don't know about the others. I'll find out.'

I thought of him, this young man I didn't know from
Adam, this dead boy with my eyes, lying in the lonely earth

or still on the chill slab of a hospital morgue, and the tears welled. Cold: all his life had been beset by it. He had been conceived of an old man's cynical lust and born of a young girl's fear. There seemed to have been some warmth in his raising, though it was a commercial undertaking, but not much of it had entered his soul. In that sunny southern land he had managed always to find cold hearts and cold minds, and to die meaninglessly in a cold desert. Whatever he had been, however little he had made of the chances he had been given, he shouldn't have had to live and die so very much alone.

Struggling both to find the words and to get them out, I stumbled: 'I want to say goodbye, Joshua. I want to make my peace with him. If he's been buried I'll visit his grave; if there's going to be a funeral I want to be there. And if he's still lying in a refrigerated box in some hospital basement I want to see him. I know it's too late to make any difference to him. But I need it. I need to say I'm sorry.'

Joshua Cade looked as though he didn't know what to do with his hands. It seemed to me that all his instincts, rooted in the emotional generosity of a peasant past, told him to put his arms round me and wait for my tears to dampen his shoulder, and if I had been his sister or his sister's friend, or any of these borderlanders who were his people, that's what he would have done, giving quiet comfort to us both. But his head told him I was a foreigner, a woman older than he from a distant, older and less spontaneous world, and he was afraid of offending me. It wasn't rejection but it felt like it.

I stood up, and sniffed once, and smiled so he wouldn't see the hurting, and I went out to my car and drove out of Sarajevo into the hills – these cold hard hills with their smugglers' trails and their ancient memories – and I got about five miles before the surging grief overtook me, obscuring the dirt road I had somehow found myself on and making it unsafe to continue.

I stopped then and, alone in the hills where he had died

– if not here then a place very like here – I wept for my brother Cristóbal as I did not remember weeping for my father or even my mother.

I hadn't told Cade where I was staying but he found me anyway. He must have worked his way through the phonebook until he came to this scrubby little motel with its mock Indian decor and its piped music. It called itself the Paramount. I found myself looking out for Norman Bates in a beaded headband.

After not sleeping much I ate practically no breakfast in my room, and I had my hand on the phone to call Cade when a horn like a rutting walrus blew under my window and it was him calling for me. I went out to meet him.

By way of greeting he said quietly, 'He's at the hospital.'

His car was a slightly up-market version of the jeeps used for the patrols. I let myself in at the passenger door. Cade watched without speaking while I strapped myself in – the adjustment on the seatbelt was stiff, as if no one ever used it. He mistook my difficulty for hesitation.

'Annie, you don't need to do this. Any arrangements that need making I can make; anything you want to know I can tell you. You don't have to look for your brother in the face of a dead stranger.'

Anger surged in me: real flaming anger, outrage, but I didn't so much shout at him as hiss. 'You arrogant bastard! How dare you? This is my family we're talking about. I've thrown up my job, spent good money and travelled six thousand miles for this, and mostly what I don't need is your opinion. You don't want to drive me, I'll drive myself. You don't want to come in, I'll find my own way. I've been doing it since I was fifteen, one more time isn't going to break me. But if you do want to come you'd better get this thing moving, because I have wasted enough time.'

He sat a moment longer looking at me; not exactly staring, not exactly smiling, his expression subtly between and compounding the two. Then he put the car in gear.

'I'm sorry if I've upset you. I'll drive you to Leyton, and I'll come in the hospital with you, and I'll bring you back; and I won't speak unless I'm spoken to, much less venture any opinions. In return there's one small thing you can do for me. Don't call me a bastard, my mother doesn't like it.'

Cade smiled and I giggled: the easing of tension between us was a good thing. I said, 'I'm sorry. I do appreciate what you're doing. And my apologies to Mrs Cade.'

The smile quickened into a grin of unexpected but unmistakable mischief. 'Miss Cade. You're not the only one who went her own way at fifteen. As long as I can remember her battle-cry has been, "They can call me a whore if they want to but they're never gonna call my son a bastard." She wanted me to be a doctor, for that reason – the way she figures it, a professional title confers retrospective legitimacy – but I couldn't face being indoors that much. I'm something of a disappointment to her.'

I doubted it. There wasn't a woman in the history of the world who wouldn't have been proud to raise a son like Joshua Cade. I said, 'All I did was cut my hair short. I think your mum did rather better for herself.'

It was an eighty-mile drive to Leyton, most of it along hillbilly roads winding, sinuous as rivers, through the russet uplands. There was no snow here, but no signs of growth either. If you looked closely you could see something of last year's vegetation, but mostly what you could see was red rock: rock ground into sparse soil, rock blowing as gritty granular dust, as knobby sandstone outcrops and as ancient weathered domes, carved and polished by wind and frost and occasional flash-floods until all the sharp angularities were worn down and carried away. They were the unstable soil and the dust that was blowing in the wind.

But the hills could not have been as barren as they looked, because they supported farms of a kind, and on one of them Joshua Cade had grown up, under the fierce eyes of his mother and the uncritical, affectionate gaze of the brother for whom she kept house. 'Not this way, the other side of town, but the hills are the same. You can get lost in these hills, even when you've known them from a kid, because there are no landmarks. Until you come on a road or a house, you could be any place.

'We had a neighbour, lived about eight miles away. One day his mule up and died, and my uncle sold him one of ours. For two months afterwards, regular as clockwork every Saturday night, that mule brought him visiting. Turned out for the last eleven years he'd relied on his old mule to take him home when he was drunk, and he couldn't understand why the new mule wouldn't do the same. Swore my uncle had sold him a bum steer.'

We laughed but I was surprised. After all, he wasn't an old man remembering his childhood. 'Do people still keep mules here?'

'Oh yes. Except it's the other way round – the mules keep the people. Well, horses mostly, but there's some jobs a mule can do better, and you can keep them on grazing that would turn a horse belly-up inside a month. Why, don't you have mules in England?'

I managed not to snap at him, but the habit goes deep. 'I don't live in England, I live in Wales. And no, we don't really. We have Welsh mountain ponies' – I waved a hand at shoulder level to indicate height – 'and Welsh cobs' – indicating breadth, I stuck one hand out of the window and threatened Cade with the other – 'but mostly we have Land Rovers and old Morris vans.'

Cade lifted up his eyes unto his hills with reverence and love. 'Up there, even this wouldn't get more than a couple of miles. Off-road you need more than four-wheel drive – you need four feet, else sooner or later your stock's going to wander off where you can't follow. Horses and helicopters – that's what keeps these hills productive. With tractors and trucks all you could farm would be a mile strip each side of the road. And there aren't many roads.'

At the morgue, a discreet annex behind the hospital, a young man in a white coat showed me to a television screen. I wasn't at my best and brightest, and somehow I thought it was to keep me amused while he got his patient ready to receive visitors. I grinned, somewhat feebly, at Cade. 'Tom and Jerry?'

'No,' he said gently, and explained.

But it wasn't what I wanted, what I had come six thousand miles for. If I had wanted snapshots, the prison in Monterrey probably had one of him – not in great shape, perhaps, but at least alive. Bureaucracy and the miracle of the deep freeze had given me an unlooked-for opportunity to do better, and I wanted to take it.

'No,' I said. 'I want to see him.'

The young man in the white coat said, 'The screen – '

'Screen be damned,' I snapped. 'This is my brother we're talking about, and I've never seen him before, and tomorrow or next week or whenever you get your paperwork sorted out you'll bury him, and the last of him will be gone. I want to see him, and I want to see him now.'

But he wasn't there. All that was there in the cold room when they pulled out the tray and zipped open the bag inside was the dead body of a stranger. It was a boy's body, slender and somehow insubstantial despite that earth-bound leadenness which is the final property of the dead; and though God knows twenty-seven years isn't much living, he didn't look he'd had even that. He didn't look he'd had enough to eat, or enough of anything except maybe hard weather – he was surprisingly brown, even in the pallor of his death. His face was brown, broad across the eyes and narrow in the jaw, and his hair was black and fine and very straight. It was too tidy, as if his mother was still combing it for him. There was no expression that I could see, only that massive complacency with which the dead regard the living.

And there was no sense at all of kinship, no feeling in my heart or in my gut that this was part of my blood, my brother whose life had been stolen. I was sorry – of course I was sorry – that a young man had died, violently and needlessly, in the cause of lining his murderer's pocket; but I could look at his sad still body on a mortuary tray and find no way of feeling his loss personally. The grieving which had enveloped me in the Sarajevo hills had gone– another bereavement, because there had been comfort in it, relief in the very violence which shook me then. Now it was too late, and the wrong place, and the body in the bag was after all a stranger, a young man who had been no more part of my life than I had been of his. It had been a conceit to think otherwise.

Cade had been right: I should not have come. I should have ended it in those bleak and barren hills, crying in the wind, where I had felt close to him and there was no stranger's face to come between us. Cade had been right and I had been wrong, and my brother Cristóbal was gone, and I could not summon him from the dead thing on the tray as I had called him up from the wind. I had lost him utterly.

We drove back to Sarajevo, and I don't think either Cade or I said a word. A couple of times he looked to me, covertly, for some kind of response but I could make none. I was feeling nothing. In all those miles only one thought came close to touching me: that I hadn't even noticed his green Welsh eyes that were like mine.

5

I slept most of the afternoon, tossing fitfully on the cheap and nasty motel bed, and woke in the early evening with my head filled with one certainty – that *nobody* notices the eyes of a corpse. Cade had lied to me. Either he had met my brother before, or Cristóbal had been alive when they found him. When Cade found him.

A kind of rage rose through me. I didn't know what it

meant, except that he had lied to me. There had to be a reason. Conceivably, as a government employee, he was acting under government instructions. That made it more, not less, incomprehensible. What possible interest could the US government have in misleading me as to the circumstances of my brother's death? I was a British citizen, he a Mexican – neither of us could matter enough to be worth lies. The other possibility was that Cade was acting not on orders but from self-interest. If so he knew more about Cristóbal than just the colour of his eyes.

I called his office. He had left for the day. I asked for – no, demanded – his home number: they offered to tell him I was looking for him, if they could locate him. 'Bloody do that,' I snapped, slamming the phone down.

I waited for it to ring, or for him to come. I wondered briefly if I should be concerned for my safety, but I couldn't feel threatened: whatever was going on in Joshua Cade's mind, it wasn't violence. He was a gentle man.

But it wasn't Cade who came. At the end of half an hour there was a quiet tap at the door, and I opened it to a cowboy.

Well no, not exactly a cowboy, it wasn't a horse he had outside but an old blue pick-up, and he wasn't wearing a stetson. But the sheepskin coat was more for warmth than fashion, the faded jeans were cut loose enough for riding, and the scuffed boots had low but pronounced heels.

Even more than his clothes, his face was right – the right slightly hawkish shape, the right weatherbeaten colour, the proper creases and just a smattering of small, interesting scars sprinkled between the infrequently shaven jaw and the slightly long, slightly lank dark brown hair. Also, the eyes narrowed correctly. If he had been three inches taller he'd have been worth a fortune to Warner Brothers.

He said, 'Can I come in?' and his voice was low, with an indeterminate drawl of an accent.

'Who are you? What do you want?'

'Call me Chico.' He said it as if he'd practised. I inferred it wasn't his name. 'I want to talk about your brother.'

It had been a rough day for me, washing between grief and fury and desolation, and I was at a pretty low ebb; but I still wasn't a push-over for the first man to swagger up to my door in high heels. I stood my ground, raised an eyebrow. 'My brother David?'

He looked surprised at that. His eyes widened, and for a moment they met mine instead of glancing by my left ear. Then he looked away again and said, 'Cristóbal Baez.'

From the way he said it he was a Spanish speaker. Most Americans, given a Mexican name to say, pronounce all the syllables with equal and undue emphasis, and manage to work a note of derision in there somewhere as well – much as the English say Angharad Meredith, or the Welsh would say Patrick O'Flaherty. Chico said it without awkwardness, without inflection, with only a small sardonic twist of his lip that was for me.

Unwithered, and declining to be rushed into what could still be a bad move, I looked him up and down – slowly, taking the time to think. 'So what do you know about Cristóbal?'

'That's what I'm here to tell you.' I could feel him getting twitchy, hear it in his voice. 'Listen, if I promise not to rape you, can we go inside? – it's cold out here, and anyhow I don't want to discuss this with half Texas.'

I leaned forward in the doorway and looked both ways, but there was no one in sight. Of course, the cigar-store Indian on the corner could have been bugged. But what the hell, answers were what I had come for, I wasn't getting many – at least not true ones – from Cade, and in the early evening in a respectable if naff motel I felt competent to deal with a shortish cowboy, whatever his motives. When a girl's first suitors are drawn from her brother's rugby club, she quickly learns to deal with a maul by means of a quick up-and-over, and ruck you Taffy. Without wishing to boast, I can claim to have played my part in the remarkable ability of Welsh forwards to run very fast while bent double. So I stood back and let him in.

There was only one chair, ostensibly upholstered in an Indian blanket. I gestured him to it with an inclination of the head while I turned again to the telephone. Partly I wanted the coffee, and partly I wanted someone to be coming round here in a few minutes with the tray.

Before I realised he had moved, his hand closed on mine, not fiercely but firm. I was about to launch into my anti-scrum procedure, but what he said and how he said it stopped me. He said, very quietly and with hardly a trace of the cowboy drawl, 'If you do that you'll endanger us both.'

I looked round at him, startled. He took his hand away and stepped back. So, after a moment, did I. I didn't understand what he had said, but I believed him. I sat down on the bed, a shade heavily, as if the shock had settled around my knees. Chico ignored the chair but perched on the edge of the writing-table, close by the window; even as we talked I knew he had one eye and one ear tuned to the dusty lot outside.

I said, 'If it's so dangerous for you to be seen here, what about your' – I hunted for the American word for pick-up, finally remembered it *was* an American word – 'pick-up?'

He shrugged and smiled, a fleeting, oddly innocent smile. 'It's not my pick-up.'

'Then whose?'

'Town mechanic's. Anyone sees it, they'll figure you needed your car looked at.'

'You want me to put the bonnet – hood– up?'

'No; nor to go round telling people who don't ask. A pick-up in a parking lot doesn't need explaining. But I don't want to be seen with you.'

He didn't mean it how it sounded, but I still didn't understand what he did mean. I gave up trying. 'Did you know Cristóbal?'

'We worked at the same job. Yeah, I knew him.'

I talk faster than I think. It has always been a problem of

mine, reacting from brain and gut and not giving my heart and soul time to get a word in edgeways. I wish I'd had a pound for every time I've said something cruel because I was clever enough to think of it and too bloody stupid to keep it to myself. I did it again now. 'Last job of his I heard about he was working as a hooker.'

That hit him harder, and hurt him more, than anything I could have done with my knee. His eyes kindled, his nostrils flared and under the tan his face flushed darkly. His voice was rough. 'You ever gone hungry, lady? Well, try it sometime, see how fastidious you feel then.'

So he had known about my brother, and not only known but cared. I sighed wearily. 'Oh, I'm sorry. I've had a funny kind of a day. You came here to tell me something. What was it?'

'You were looking for Cade.'

'So how come I got you?'

He grinned. His grin was a lot less innocent than his smile, only in part because he was still angry. 'Cade had a funny kind of a day too.'

I found myself chuckling. It was that or thump him. 'While he's recovering, why don't you tell me why you're here?'

He looked out of the window, between the slats of the anachronistic blind, eyes focusing softly on the middle distance, not because there was anything there to concern him but because that way he could avoid looking at me without making an issue of it. He said, 'To ask you to go home, before your questions and your presence attract enough attention to get me or someone like me killed.'

He had my attention now. He checked that with a scant sidelong glance and went on. 'Your brother was someone like me. They killed him, and they killed six other men to make sure, and people that ruthless will kill anyone they think can threaten them. That includes me; conceivably, it could include you.

'Your brother wasn't a waster and he wasn't a wetback.

He was an agent of the United States government tasked
with tracing the pipelines that bring in Mexican illegals.
We trace them and the Federal authorities close them
down, and the operators mostly go to ground before we
can get at them, and open up someplace else. And when a
few of them get their heads together they exchange
profiles on the agents they've passed down the line, and
next time one shows up they kill him. That's what
happened to Chris.'

I hadn't guessed. I felt then that I should have, but I
hadn't even suspected. I groped to make sense of it. 'But –
he was in jail. He robbed someone – an antiques dealer – '

Chico smiled. 'A smuggler of unlicensed artifacts. He was
already working for us then. We knew the man smuggled
historical treasures across the border for the benefit of
wealthy American collectors – we figured he probably
smuggled drugs and illegals as well. Turning his place over
was a calculated risk that didn't quite pay off – at least, not
as we'd expected. It turned out OK, though, because after
leaving your brother to stew for a couple of months behind
bars, where he had just enough influence to keep the
pressure up, the guy offered to get him out if Chris would
work for him. He thought a scared half-breed hood on the
run from the law was just what his business needed. We
thought Christmas had come.'

'That was six years ago. He lived like that for six years?'

'Hell, no. We wrapped that one up after about four
months. That guy didn't open up again under name: he
got twelve years, one thing with another.'

'And Cristóbal got only six.'

He looked at me almost sharply for a moment, then
nodded. 'I guess. But he did some good work before they
got him. Cade'll tell you that. He must have crossed that
border fifty times, on foot and in trucks and twice on
horseback, and most every time he closed them down.
There's a lot of men doing time because of his work, and a
lot of Mexican families making the best of a hard time at

home instead of paying every penny they have to some hood who'd scatter them all over the southern states, get most of them robbed and some of them killed, and count his profits while US Immigration deports half his clients and US businessmen feed on the rest.'

'Is that why you do it? For the Mexicans?' Like Cade, he seemed too anxious to justify himself.

For a moment, like Cade, there was something haunted, something guilty in his eyes. 'I don't know. Christ, I hope so. I hope we're right. Some of them make good lives here, you know? They pay their way, they take work Americans won't do, they don't make any trouble. I hope the bastards bringing them up aren't right and Immigration wrong all along.'

There was almost nothing left to say. I said, 'Listen, thanks for coming. It makes a kind of sense now.'

'Cade never could lie to save his life.'

I smiled. 'Not just what he told me. My brother's life. It seemed such an incredible waste. It's still a waste, but at least he achieved something. I thought he had died because half his family didn't care if he lived and the other half didn't even know he existed. You've no idea what a relief it is to know it wasn't neglect that killed him.'

I felt him watching me and forced a laugh. 'You think I'm crazy.'

'No.'

'It's just, I'm glad he managed to make himself a life worth having. Chico, you knew him. Was he happy?'

'Happy?' He said it as if the very concept was alien to him, as if it would never have occurred to him to wonder; as if his voice would have run up in the same bewildered incredulity if someone had asked about his happiness. But he recovered, pushing his voice down again with some small embarrassment. 'Will you settle for satisfied?'

I nodded. Happy was an outright win, but satisfied was better than a draw.

He was ready to leave. He checked outside through the

slats of the blind, separated delicately with fingers as strong and precise as a musician's. He rose from the table in a slow fluid movement like a stretching cat. But he still didn't look at me. 'You'll go home then?'

'I suppose so. I haven't had much time to think about it. I wanted there to be something I could do here.'

'There's nothing you can do.'

'No. Well, I suppose I might as well leave, then. I might go down into Mexico for a little while.'

'In God's name, why?'

I was surprised by his vehemence and stared at him. 'Whyever not? My father loved Mexico: he left a child there, and all the time he was home he was wishing he was back. I was raised on his stories about Mexico, chose my career because of them: I may know more about Mexican history than anybody you've ever met, but I've never seen the bloody place. Until yesterday, when I ate a meal there. Now I have the time and the opportunity to see the place, you want me out of here and there's nothing to hurry home for. Why shouldn't I take a run down?'

'I told you, we have work to do and you're in the way.'

I felt myself getting nettled. 'Listen, kid, I'm trying to be reasonable here. It's a big country and you can't possibly be working in all of it. How about Yucatan? I have a friend – well, an acquaintance – working there, I'll maybe take a run down and see him.'

The cowboy was getting heated too. 'They like to tell you down there that the border isn't Mexico and Mexico isn't the border. But it is, because there's nowhere you can go that the politics of the border don't follow. Anywhere you go down there, there'll be someone who knows your brother was a US agent; and if you get yourself into difficulties you can't get out of, it'll be your brother's colleagues who have the task of extracting you. Lady, you could get people killed.'

'And when I've seen Richard,' I went on, pointedly ignoring him, 'I've some family business in Veracruz. I thought I'd try and track down Señorita Baez, introduce myself – tell her that the old man is dead, and now their kid is too; see if she remembers either of them.'

He was clearly shocked. Everything about him was open-mouthed except his mouth, which was pinched shut by bloodless lips. His eyes were appalled. The cat had his tongue. Finally he managed, 'I don't think I like you very much, Miss Meredith.'

I elevated an eyebrow at him. 'I'll try and live with the upset.'

He left without another word. I heard his pick-up start grumpily and drive away. I watched the bead curtain behind the door tremble to a standstill, feeling like a rat. I'd done it again: shocked someone not by speaking my mind, which I'm prepared to do, or even my heart, but just by exercising my face for the pleasure of the sounds coming out of it. I hadn't meant it. It was my parents I was angry with, and they were dead, not Cristóbal's mother whose only crime was that she had been too young to cope with what life had thrown at her.

But anger – mine, anyway – is like water and finds its own level, even if it wreaks turbulent havoc in the process. I blame my Celtic ancestors: there was no mildness bred among those rugged hills.

When the beads fell silent I pulled out my suitcase and began to pack.

6

To this day I am unsure which way I would have travelled – south to Yucatan or north to the airport – had the matter ended there. I think I would have gone into Mexico and damned the consequences, and probably there would have been no consequences. But Chico's departure, to the chink of beads and the growl of an elderly engine, was the end of nothing. An hour later headlights swung across my

window – the red hills outside had fallen into darkness –
and a red-headed girl presented herself at my door with an
invitation.

She was tall, not just taller than me, and about twenty
years old, and she said her name was Savannah Mason.
The invitation was from her father.

'We're having a kind of party up at the Valley
tomorrow.' She grinned, handsomely. 'Daddy has some
new toys from Guatemala he wants to show off. It'll be
mostly family and friends, but Daddy thought – since
you're alone in Sarajevo and if you're interested in
archaeology – you might like to come along too. If you've
nothing else planned.'

'The Valley?'

'Sugar Valley – it's our house. You take the River Road
and then – oh hell, anyone round here can put you right
for the Valley. Or just pick a car and follow it – half the
town's coming. Or maybe you'd like a ride up? – come to
that, I can run down for you myself, it's no distance. Say
about four?'

She'd said it all without pausing for breath, and could
clearly have said more if she'd had more to say. She had
one of those wide mouths that go with red hair, and
freckles over the bridge of her nose, and she talked in a
gush of a Texas accent that suggested that nothing quite as
exciting and jolly had ever happened as this party up at
Sugar Valley. She no doubt sounded just the same buying
onions and paying her paperbill. The twinkle in her hazel
eyes reached all the way down to her hidden but assuredly
manicured toenails.

My first impression was that she was stunning. On
second thoughts I decided she was actually rather vacuous
but that men would find her stunning. Finally I came to
the conclusion that she *was* stunning, and the vacuity was a
cover, a kind of satire.

I said, 'What sort of new toys from Guatemala?'

She looked amazed, the great hazel eyes saucering.

Then she grinned again. 'Hey, I'm sorry, it's just that we don't see too many strangers round here and everyone in Sarajevo knows about Daddy's toys. He collects old things – just about anything old, even his car is one of your Rolls-Royces' – *my* Rolls-Royces? – 'from 1933. But mostly he collects pre-Columbian art. Statues, figurines, carvings – he's even got a Peruvian mummy! He heard you were an historian and he'd really love to show you his collection.'

'Does he also know why I'm here?'

Her face fell still at that, all its animation quieted, but her eyes didn't flinch. She nodded. 'Because of your half-brother. Listen, if I'm intruding I'm sorry. I didn't mean to upset you. Maybe it was pretty tactless, but – We just didn't want you to feel you were alone here. I'm sorry; I'll go.'

'OK,' I said. She turned back to her car, fumbling for the door-handle in her embarrassment. I called after her, 'Four-thirty be time enough?'

She spun round, grinning from ear to ear. 'Do fine. You're driving up? – find something ostentatious on the River Road and follow it. Or ask anyone for Raoul Mason's Sugar Valley. You can't miss it.'

Well no; not passing over at forty thousand feet in a jumbo jet could you have missed Sugar Valley. In a cleft of the red hills it was a slash of emerald and white. the paddocks were obviously watered by some means ancillary to the little rushing stream foaming over the rocks beside the drive, because they spread out to maybe half a mile on each side and at the last white-painted fence they gave way immediately to arid scrubland again.

The paddocks were stocked with horses: not working horses such as Cade had talked about but classy, valuable animals. Most of them were Quarter horses, built shorter and more substantial than a Thoroughbred, with a breedy front end and enormous power behind the saddle for the vital start in two-furlong races. They were different shades of brown. The other horses were Appaloosas, flecked and spotted in a seemingly infinite range of patterns, and underneath the brushwork every one of them reassuringly common. I couldn't count how many there were in all; there might have been half a hundred. They represented a lot of work and a lot of wealth.

Up ahead, where the stream tumbled out of the hills, the drive continued for another hundred yards, flanked by white rails, then took a broad sweep round to the right in front of the house. Or perhaps not so much a house as a hacienda. It was broad and white under a pantile roof. It looked low, but only because it spread so far. The whole of the second storey was distinguished at the front by a balcony, and the main double doorway on the ground floor was approached by a wide curve of steps and guarded by a colonnaded portico.

Shrubs in big wooden tubs grew green under the large segmented windows. The tubs were an affectation, because clearly the plants weren't moved indoors in the winter. Nor was there much need to: the temperature in the little valley, sheltered all round by sun-absorbing hills, was perceptibly higher than it had been down on the River Road. Somehow it seemed natural, as if the wealth which had colonised this valley, built that house, bred those horses, should also find a way of purchasing a preferential climate. I should not have been surprised to learn that, in the blazing heat of the summer, while Sarajevo sweated and the river parched and the hills ran to dust, Sugar Valley's guardian heights contrived to feed the stream, shade the house and send down the occasional cooling breeze.

Savannah Mason met me on the steps, complete with a uniformed flunky who hastened to drive my car out of sight. I didn't really blame him: it was a respectable and reliable car but it wasn't chosen, or indeed designed, with social occasions like this one in mind. Momentarily embarrassed, I started to apologise. 'I'm sorry I had nothing more suitable to come in ... '

Savannah, who showed every sign of growing on one in much the same way as the athlete's foot fungus, took my coat, patted the sleeve of my best party frock reassuringly and said, 'You look fine.'

Anyway, the flunky was driving everybody's car out of sight. He must have reckoned signs of life would spoil the architectural vista.

At the top of the steps, through the big double doors, opened a square hall, white-walled and terrazzo-tiled, big enough to entertain all Sarajevo and tall enough for them to bring their giraffes. The hall rose through both storeys, with a gallery round where the staircase reached the landing. On the ground floor there were three doors, all of them open, clusters of people talking too loudly and laughing at too little beyond. One was evidently the living-room, one the dining-room; the third, at the back of the house, appeared to be some kind of conservatory, for tropical green flared behind the talking heads.

But I felt no inclination to move through and investigate, not yet. For the moment the gay social whirl could circulate without me. In the hall there was treasure.

I use the word advisedly. I've a few nice things myself, including a few pieces of meso-American art, and I like to keep them around for my own enjoyment and that of people who call. If I didn't I would keep them in a shoebox under my bed. It's the same with most historians – those who still have some purchasing power after paying the milk bill, anyway.

But this was something different. I've seen good museums – important museums, not just collections of old junk in a back room of the town hall – which couldn't mount a display of pre-Columbian artifacts to rival what I could see in this rich man's hall. I know good museums which would have blown their entire budget by purchasing any one of these items, and would have gone ahead and blown it and spent the curator's salary as well, except that after you've found the goods and after you've found the money you still have to get export permits and even good museums can have difficulties with this quality of exhibit. Mr Mason must have begun collecting as a very young man, before the legal requirements became an obstacle.

Displayed on the walls were not one or two but several quipu, those fringes of knotted cords by which the Inca civil service stored information on their extensive empire. The colours were still distinct, the knots in place. Atahualpa's chancellor, woken from his four-hundred-and-fifty-year sleep, would have known instantly just how many bushels of grain were owed in tax by, say, the nobles at Tampu Machay to the Sapa Inca at Cuzco.

In glass cases at eye-level were a pair of aryballus pots, found with Inca burials, and an Olmec axe topped by a grotesque face and worked in pearly grey jadeite from the mines at Oaxaca in the mountains south of Veracruz. A Haida mask, born of the ancestor cult practised in the Queen Charlotte Islands, surveyed the proceedings with knowingness and humour from above the conservatory door.

There were other things which I struggled to identify: Peruvian pottery from the Mochica and Chimu peoples, and Chancay pottery figurines; Toltec Mazapan bowls and gold and silver ornaments from the Mixmec of Monte Alban. On the fringes of my knowledge were pots and basketwork from the desert cultures of the American border states.

But no special knowledge was needed to identify the centrepiece of the display. 3b back home could have identified it; well, by the time they'd had me a year they could. It was a Mayan stele, and if it wasn't from Copán it was from somewhere very close. It was superb. It was a pillar of stone, twice my height, square in cross-section, and every inch of every facet was covered with deeply inscribed carving. The front of the stone, facing the door, carried the likeness of a man – a moon-faced man with incongruously large ears, with his bare feet spread and his hands clasped before him as if to support the weight of the bracelets on his arms. His clothes were ornate, every fold and every decoration faithfully sculpted, and his head-dress was an awesome confection of masks and feathers towering perhaps a third of the statue's height.

Because statue was what it was. The Maya never developed wholly three-dimensional art, but the relief on their stelae grew in time so profound that, coupled with their treatment of the reverse and flanking facets, these megaliths took on the appearance and the role and to all intents and purposes the significance of free-standing statuary. The stelae were to the pyramid city of Copán what the colossi were to the temples at Karnak.

And to a private collector of pre-Columbian artifacts – even a very rich collector – such a stele represented an impossible dream. However early in life he had begun collecting, it seemed inconceivable that Mr Mason had obtained his stele by admissible means. Yet here it was, on virtually public display in the front hall of the man's house, where casual callers – if he had such things – were not likely but absolutely certain to see it. The answer was, of course, that they were meant to, just as I was. It was a plain statement, even a challenge. What it said was that wealth was power – perhaps not absolute power, but sure as hell enough.

I whispered hoarsely to Savannah, 'How in the name of all that's holy – ?' and found myself looking into the amused expression of her father. Not that anyone introduced us. There was no need.

Raoul Mason was inches shorter than his daughter, which still didn't put him in my league but made communication between us possible. He was also dark where she was fair: Savannah's mother must have been the all-time all-American golden girl. Her father was of French extraction, the clue of the Christian name confirmed by the black hair swept back from a widow's peak at his brow and trimmed elegantly to a pointed beard.

His skin was dark in tone but fine in texture, not swarthy, and his eyes were dark blue, almost navy blue, brim-full with meanings. Right now, in a scrupulously polite way, they were laughing at me.

'How did the old son of a bitch get that? Was that your question, Miss Meredith?' The lips were smiling too, now, and there was a melodious note of humour in the unexpectedly bass voice.

I recovered quickly enough to smile back and not apologise. 'Actually, how come it isn't in the basement surrounded by broken floorboards?'

Mason laughed, the deep rich tolling of a bell. 'Steel piles underneath carry the weight down to bedrock. If he goes through the floor, he won't stop this side of Korea.'

A butler approached with a tray of glasses. Mason lifted two, without asking what I wanted. It was champagne: French, not Californian. We toasted one another.

'But since you raise the subject,' I went on smoothly, 'how did you come by it?'

'I bought it.'

'You bought a Copán stele?'

One elegant eyebrow elevated appreciatively. 'You do know your subject. He is indeed from Copán. But that's not where I bought him.'

'Then where?'

His smile broadened, even coarsened. There was enormous arrogance in the red curve of those full lips, framed by the perfectly sculpted beard. 'From a whorehouse in the Mojave desert. Should I explain?'

'I really think you'd better.'

'The place used to be on one of the main trucking routes into the south-west. It was a gold-mine. They had the stele outside the front door, like a sign. I think the shape of it appealed to them. I won't tell you what they called the establishment. Then a new road was opened: it was straighter and it was faster, and it left the regular clientele speeding across the desert twenty miles away. In time all that were left were some tumbledown buildings and the stele. I bought the place. I sold the buildings to the Eagle Scouts for a boys' camp. It seemed not altogether inappropriate.'

I forbore to comment. 'And before it was a free-standing advertisement for a house of ill-repute in the Mojave desert?'

'Copán, certainly. I have provenance. How or when he came north I have no idea. I have no reason to question his bona fides as part of the property which I purchased.'

It was quite possible. For a long time after the jungle cities were rediscovered, much of the region was in the hands of local bandits and corrupt administrators. If the treasures found there were not theirs, nobody cared to tell them so, and undoubtedly they sold many priceless artifacts to curious, wealthy and occasionally erudite travellers whose subsequent title to the goods could hardly be disproved. Mason's stele could well have been such a case. And yet I felt uneasy.

No such question-mark hung over the new toys from Guatemala. They were attractive but unremarkable pieces of gold and silver jewellery; he had acquired them through the usual channels and took, it seemed, a mischievous pleasure in showing me the paperwork to prove it. He was teasing me but also, just a little, he was testing me.

Very, very gently, and more from a casual malice than any genuine interest, I began testing him back. 'All the same, it must be galling – to you as a serious collector, I mean.'

'What must?'

'The amount of red tape. Oh, maybe it's necessary; certainly nobody would want to see great national treasures exported into private collections. But an awful lot of stuff simply doesn't come into that category. It could be earning valuable dollars, and giving immense pleasure, and no one any the worse off.'

'I'm inclined to agree with you,' murmured Mason, his

eyes on my face.

'And for another thing,' I went on, warming to the role of devil's advocate, 'look at this place.' We stood together in the middle of the hall, revolving slowly, looking at it. 'These things are beautiful here, and they're cared for. You have the knowledge and the resources – let's be honest, the money – to conserve what you collect. They're safer here than where they came from.'

'Many people, and many scholars among them' – he made a small bow, smiling the compliment my way – 'would argue that they should be on public display.'

'In an ideal world, where such people – scholars among them – were prepared to put their hands deep enough into their pockets to pay for it, so would I. In the meantime collectors are finding, preserving and protecting these things for a possibly more enlightened future.'

His smile had grown almost radiant, the smile of a man hearing what he wanted to hear. 'You're right, of course. It comes down to money. Bankrupt and virtually bankrupt central American governments have higher priorities than the conservation and display of old things, and with dying children on their streets you cannot blame them. But these things die too: neglect, and ignorance even more, kill them. I'd like to think the time will come, when these countries have sorted out their economic problems, that they'll be grateful to collectors for preserving cores of important work abroad.'

'You'd break up your collection to sell them back these things?'

The smile went impish round the corners. 'Well, no, perhaps I wouldn't. But maybe Savannah will when they're hers. They'll still be here then. Hell, there'll be more of them then.' And with that he steered me off to meet his mummy.

He had other guests, of course, but he must have counted them friends enough to bear a little neglect. We had supper together in the conservatory, then he conducted me over the contents of the display cabinets in his private study beyond which was not part of the general tour. He was a man not lacking in subtlety: he left the door ajar, but the room was sufficiently removed from the party that the sounds of talking and laughter reached us only huskily and there was no one to interrupt. His voice, always deep, dropped another tone.

'While we are alone, Miss Meredith, I should like to offer you my sympathy on the tragedy that brought you here.'

I had thought I was coping with it: well enough to bully Joshua Cade, even well enough to make bad taste jokes about it to his friend Chico. But that unexpected expression of kindness hit me right in the gut. My throat knotted, my eyes brimmed: all I could do was nod in what I hoped was a gracious fashion and pray he wouldn't press it. If I had to speak my voice would break in a million pieces.

Mason saw my distress and something like remorse rose through him, lifting his hands and shoulders in helpless gestures and twisting his face. 'Oh Angharad, I am sorry! I only intended – And now I've upset you. Forgive me – please?'

I had to say something. 'Of course.' It came out too loud, scratchy, about as graceful as a belch. I tried again. 'Of course. Please don't apologise. You've been very kind. It's just – it still smarts when the air gets at it.'

We didn't go back to the party at once. He found a bottle and some fresh glasses, and we sat in his study – sharing a big leather settee, the drinks on a low table before us – and sipped and talked. We talked about his hobby and his house, and his wife – Savannah's mother, who had died leaving him an eight-year-old child to bring up – and we talked about Cristóbal.

I told him what I had learnt, without telling him how, about my brother's work for the government. It had become a matter of pride, that people who thought he had died a penniless wetback should know different. 'You wouldn't believe what a shock that was, when I thought I knew how he'd been living and why he died. I mean, it was a relief too, because it meant he hadn't spent all his days in poverty and despair, but somehow it made the waste worse, made the hurting worse. He deserved better than to die like that, and I never knew him but I miss him like hell.'

'You went to the hospital, I understand.'

'Joshua Cade took me. It seemed – important.'

'I think it is important. When we lose someone, part of our mind does anything it can to reject the loss. Intellectually we know, but emotionally there remains a kind of doubt. Going there, seeing him, would settle that doubt.'

'Yes,' I agreed slowly, 'that was it. That was how it was.' I wondered at his understanding. 'It was only then I stopped expecting someone to leap up suddenly and say there'd been a mistake.'

A little while afterwards we went back to the party, and soon after that, exhausted all at once with the day's events, I made my excuses and left. Mason left his other guests to see me down the broad steps, and the uniformed flunky brought my homely car. We shook hands, with courtesy but also some empathy, and I got in my car and drove away.

It was quite dark, no moon showing in the broad track of sky between the hills, and the valley seemed shrunk to a ribbon of gravel road flanked by palings brilliant in my headlights. There was the brief rattle of a timber bridge where the stream ducked under the drive, and then the tall white gates, closed now, threw fretwork reflections back at me. I slowed down, waiting for someone to open them.

Then I saw that they wouldn't be opened for a moment yet because the gateman was otherwise engaged: engaged, with two friends, in beating the living daylights out of Cade's friend Chico.

Chico

1

I had clearly missed the best bit, the bit where Chico was fighting back. It must have been good, because one of his adversaries was still sitting in the roadway, oblivious of the blinding headlights, holding himself and gently rocking. The gateman, too, had had a busy evening: the cheek below his eye was cut like a boxer's, and blood had poured from his nose down over his mouth and chin. His uniform, what I could see of it, was rumpled and stained with road dirt, but I couldn't see it all because he was holding Chico in front of him like a shield while the third man powered measured blows like morningstars into the cowboy's midriff.

He wasn't fighting any more. The man behind him held his arms without difficulty. His knees were buckled, if they had let him go he'd have gone down. His head was sunk on his chest: I only realised it was him when the man hitting him in the belly lifted his head by a handful of hair in order to hit him in the face for a change. His face was blackened and bloody, and fish-belly white in the glaring light, and there must have been something familiar about the shape of him or his clothes because his own mother would have been hard pressed to recognise his face. He was barely conscious, his eyes almost shut, just a white line showing under each lid, and he wasn't aware of me or the car or the light, only the fists and the hurting.

Gradually the other two became aware of the light. It seemed to dawn on them quite slowly that the spotlight on top of the gatepost and the overspill from the open door of the lodge had been supplemented by something else. First the man facing me looked up, squinting at me over the top of Chico's head; then the one hitting him stopped and turned round.

After a moment's hesitation I wound down the window. Incredibly, the one with his hands free walked over to the car and bent down politely to speak with me. He was going to have a black eye in the morning, and his knuckles were raw.

I said, as calmly as I could, 'Does Mr Mason know about this?'

'Not yet, miss. It's only just happened.' He was a big man with a powerful voice, but he didn't sound at all like someone with a lot of explaining to do. 'But it's happened before. It's best just to beat the crap out of them – begging your pardon, miss – and throw them out. If we catch them before they steal anything, there's nothing much to charge them with anyway. It's best just to dissuade them from coming back.'

I cleared my throat, hunting for a natural tone. 'Who is he?'

The man looked at me as if I were a harmless simpleton. 'He's a thief, miss. They come up for the parties. They try to get into the grounds so they can pick up some purses, or maybe look in a few cars. If they can't get in, sometimes they try to stop cars on the road after the party. They pretend to be sick or hurt or something, and rob you when you stop. Well, this one won't be pretending, but I don't think any of Mr Mason's regular guests will be stopping to help him.'

'Can't the police do anything about it?'

'The sheriff,' he corrected me gently, 'has more important things to do.'

I didn't know what to do. I knew Chico wasn't a thief. I also knew how much it mattered that no one found out he was a government agent. He could have told them himself, but obviously counted his cover more important than the cost of protecting it. Perhaps he hadn't expected to be hurt like this. He was long past helping himself: I was going to have to try and help him.

I nodded understanding at the big man with the black eye and the bloody fists. 'Well, I'm a stranger round here. I expect you know your own business best. Listen, chuck him out now, will you, then I can get on my way?' I waited expectantly.

He didn't think he had anything to hide, didn't see my involvement as anything but arbitrary and fringe, and saw no reason to be difficult. 'OK, miss.'

He left his friend holding up the limp body of the cowboy – without the sheepskin coat now, I noticed, on top of everything else he must have been frozen half to death – and went to throw the gates open. Then he took one of Chico's arms from his colleagues and together they heaved him out on to the highway. He rolled once and lay still. Then, more gently, the big man helped his other friend up and steered him towards the lodge. Finally, courteously, he waved me on. 'Good night, miss.'

'Good night.' I heard the gate clang shut behind me, and the men were on one side and Chico safe on the other, though he could have been dying in his blood in the gutter for all I knew. I dared not let them hear the car stop. I drove away, accelerating round the first corner on the River Road, and stopped there. I left the car idling and ran back.

Primitive instinct had driven him to escape the light. He had crawled – on his belly, the marks of it were clear in the dust beside the road – maybe a dozen yards to where a rocky outcrop, blasted for the highway, reared into the light from the gate and cast a pool of inky shadow at its foot. That was where I found him, face down in the dirt. I dropped on my knees beside him and touched him with my hand, and his whole body shook. A constant throbbing tremor like machinery ran the length of him.

But he still wasn't unconscious, just battered to an infant weakness. He reacted to my touch with a spasm of fear, curling up foetally with his arms round his head. He thought they had come back for him.

'Chico, it's all right – it's me, Annie Meredith.' I couldn't think how to hold him without hurting him.

Slowly he uncurled, and got his face off the mud, and struggled to focus his closing eyes on me. His breathing was ragged, full of blood and pain. When he recognised me he let out a tiny sob of relief. Then he growled, 'Get me out of here.'

I wanted to take him to the hospital at Leyton but he wouldn't hear of it. I was worried about the damage those big fists could have done, in his head and in his belly; he wanted only to be left alone to curl up and regather his strength. We compromised: I said I'd deliver him to Joshua Cade and let him decide what was necessary.

It was the middle of the night but I didn't know about his shifts. 'Where's he likely to be?'

'At home,' grunted Chico.

'Not at his office?'

'He said he was going home.'

'When?'

'When he dropped me at Sugar Valley.'

Chico told me where to go. Cade's house was, perhaps predictably, on the opposite side of town to Sugar Valley. We took a back road that was no more than a dirt track to avoid driving through Sarajevo. Once we met a car and Chico slid down the seat and under the dashboard. Once he nearly turned himself inside out with a paroxysm of coughing that left him exhausted and trying to hide the blood on his hands. Wordlessly I passed him my handkerchief. After a moment, also without comment, he used it.

Somewhere behind Sarajevo we found a proper road running up into the hills. A couple of miles along Chico said, 'Here,' and where the road swung to the right a track

– no more than that – branched off to the left. Almost at once the headlights shone back, reflected from the windows of a small low house that the English would call a bungalow and the Americans possibly a cabin. Cade's 4-x-4 was parked in front. A light at the side of the house spilled out on to a paddock and a small barn, perhaps for his uncle's mule. There was no other building in sight. Presuming there were no neighbours either, I stubbed the heel of my hand on the horn and kept it there until the door flung open.

Cade had been in the process of going to bed. His shirt hung open outside his belt and he was barefoot. He seemed to feel neither the cold nor the stones. His eyes swallowed me as I got out of the car. He might not have been expecting this, but he'd been expecting something. 'What happened?'

'Chico's hurt.'

I was redundant from then on. Cade looked him over, talking to him in a low businesslike monotone. Then he took Chico's arm round his shoulders and lifted him from the car, and more carried than helped him into the house. I followed them through the living-room into Cade's bedroom, the blankets on the bed turned back for the night. Cade dragged them one-handed on to the floor, eased Chico on to his back and pulled his boots off.

'Kitchen's across the way,' he said to me. 'Get some coffee on.'

'I'm not sure he should have coffee.'

'It's not for him. It's for you, and me, and Dr McQuoid, and then we'll see.'

Chico feebly batted his hands away, tried to sit up and failed. 'I don't need McQuoid.'

'I'll take his word for that, not yours.'

I heard him on the phone while I waited for the kettle to boil. I heard him swear softly.

'Problem?'

He came into the kitchen, taking cottonwool and iodine

from a cupboard and filling a basin from the big kettle. 'McQuoid's out of town.'

'There must be another doctor.'

'Not one he can use. McQuoid we can trust: anyone else could do him more damage than Mason's crew.'

When the coffee was ready I took it into the living-room and Cade joined me soon afterwards. He had buttoned his shirt but still had nothing on his feet. They were big and capable-looking, and appeared quite used to knocking round unshod.

'He'll live.' He took a mug into the bedroom.

I waited patiently for him to return, and fold into the armchair beside the fire, and reach over to pour coffee for himself. Then I said, really quite reasonably, 'What the holy hell is going on?'

Immediately he looked wary. He glanced, involuntarily, perhaps unconsciously, at the open door he had just come through, wishing he could leave the explanations to the injured man and knowing he couldn't. 'Miss Meredith, I know this is hard for you to understand – '

'If you're about to tell me all our lives are in danger, I already know that. It's why I watched those animals beat him senseless instead of telling them who he is. If no one knew about him before tonight they don't now. But *I* know what he is, and what he does, and I want to know why he followed me to Raoul Mason's. And if I don't get straight answers this time, Joshua Cade, I just might go and ask at Sugar Valley.'

I don't think he took the threat seriously, but he took me seriously. He stretched out long legs and leaned back in his chair, the mug cupped in both hands before his face as if, at least on an instinctive level, he was taking cover behind it. But his eyes were steady over the top of it and the steam.

'It wasn't you he was spying on, it was Mason. We think he's smuggling: illegals, bits of other people's history, drugs. We wanted to know who was at that party tonight, and who stayed on after the others left. I guess Chico was as surprised to see you there as you were to see him.'

My mind was racing. I was aware of inferences that I couldn't confront. Raoul Mason – the rich, the elegant, the urbane; my gracious host, my kind sympathiser; that respected man, chief among the local nobility; the man who had asked about my brother – a smuggler? It was hard to believe, yet all my instincts told me immediately that it was true. 'I knew he was lying about that stele!'

Cade laughed. 'The one from The Hard Man? Sorry to disappoint you, but that may be the one piece in his collection that he did acquire legitimately. That's why he makes such a thing of showing it off: because it seems so certain to be illegal, and because his title is so demonstrably good. He'd just love to be challenged over it.'

'Then what?'

'My guess – and it is still only a guess – is, most of the rest of it. The small pieces especially, the bits that can be hidden in the plaster on a broken arm, or folded in an executive's breast-pocket handkerchief, or stuffed inside a child's rag doll. But bigger things too. If you're bringing illegals in by truck you risk nothing extra by having a couple of tons of stone in packing cases on the floor.'

I thought of him, posing smugly in his own house before a treasure-trove of illegally imported artifacts, content for everyone to know and daring someone to prove it. For more than a passing moment I had to work hard not to admire the man. I might have been playing up to him with what I said about his collecting, but much of it was at least arguably true. All my background and training insisted that what he did was wrong as well as illegal. But there was something about the man, something about his confidence and his success, something charismatic, that suggested there was no right or wrong about it, that spoils belonged to the victor and winning was the only qualification.

Then, belatedly, what Cade had said caught up with me. 'Illegals? You think he smuggles people too?'

'That's why my department is interested in him. The

Feds care more about the drugs, and stopping unlicensed exports is strictly speaking a job for the Mexican authorities.'

I knew where this was taking us. Part of me wanted to stop it before the knowledge was irrevocably mine. But, just the same, I asked. 'And Cristóbal?'

He knew how important it was. His eyes were honest. 'We don't know, Annie, not for sure. But yes, that's what we think – that it was Mason's mules brought that truck over the border and abandoned it. That's what Chris believed when he joined that train.'

'You mean,' I said, slowly and carefully, anxious to leave no room for error, 'I spent tonight drinking wine with the man who murdered my brother?'

Cade's eyes, over the mug, cast round the room, again pausing wistfully on the bedroom door. 'I can't say that; not yet. The operation was a failure so we never traced the route. Yes, whoever ran that mule-train killed him, and it may have been Mason, and if you want my personal opinion I think it was. Whoever it was, we have not done trying to catch him. Someone else will take over your brother's job, and if there is a God in heaven, and also quite possibly if there is not, we'll succeed in connecting him with what was done to Chris and those other men, and then he'll pay. But I can't promise you it will be soon.'

'I want to help.' For a moment I couldn't think who'd said it.

Cade's eyes flared wide and wary and he started to shake his head, but it wasn't him who said, 'No.' Chico was in the bedroom door, steadying himself with a hand on the jamb. He looked even worse by electric light than he had by moonshine, his face and body patterned by welts and grazes and livid bruising. His shirt, open, hung from his shoulders as if he had shrunk since he put it on. But he was on his feet, and judging from the amount of emphasis he got into that one word, which was as much as most people could have got into a medium-sized speech, he was in command of his faculties as well. That didn't necessarily make him right.

'I can help. I can help you nail him.'

'No way. I mean it, Josh. You get her out of here and send her home.'

I shot to my feet, spitting at him. 'Neither of you has any power to send me anywhere. I go where I choose; and I'll do what I think fit. I know Mason's weakness, where he's vulnerable. I can exploit that, maybe draw him out, in a way neither of you can. If you really want to stop him, you need me and what I know about his treasures, and the fact that he sought me out to offer me friendship. He'll never accept anyone that you send to him in the way he'll trust me if I ask him to. If you cared as much about Cristóbal and those others as you keep telling me, you can't afford to refuse the chance I can offer you.'

'I can,' Chico said, with conviction.

For what seemed a long time Cade said nothing. Then: 'You have a plan?'

2

We met in Mexico City. It was neither midway nor neutral ground, but it was the best I was going to do. Balfour brought a portly smiling Mexican from the National Museum of Anthropology. I had Joshua Cade, improbably dressed in a suit, as my second.

The Mexican, whom Balfour introduced by a machine-gun battery of names that boiled down to Esteban Alvarado, took us to his office at the museum and we drew up chairs to a round table. Before he would allow us to start Alvarado, smiling, served us with dark, bitter coffee. Balfour, typically, downed his in one and scowled at me.

I was surprised – God knows why – how much older he looked. It must have been a dozen years since I'd seen him, of course, and no doubt I too had long lost the insouciance of my mid-twenties. But I don't think even 3b would have described me as worn, weary and weathered, and disappointed and sour, and unless appearances were very deceptive Richard was all of those things. He looked old beyond either of our years. His skin was darkened by sun and rain, not so much tanned as sallowed, with an unhealthy cast that suggested jungles didn't agree as well with him as with Tarzan. He hadn't shaved today, and I wasn't sure he'd washed. He looked tired and used, and not so very far from used up. Also he was smaller than I remembered, shorter and less bulky. To go with my short cowboy I had a cut-price Indiana Jones.

But his intellect was as gin-trap sharp as ever. It gleamed through his eyes, the pupils bright with a tiny, residual fever-flame, when I met his angry gaze. He resented being here, being involved in this. I hadn't given him much choice, and he resented that most of all. 'Do you want to tell me what this is all about?' The bitterness in his voice was like the coffee, and he filled his mouth with it too and swallowed it whole.

I said, 'Just across the border there's a man who has grown rich and powerful trading in unlicensed artifacts and human misery. My half-brother came close to proving it and Mason had him killed. I want him for that. I know how to get him. But I need your help.'

I explained, carefully, what I had in mind.

It would be inadequate to say he didn't like the idea. If it had been his office he would have thrown me out. But it wasn't, it was Alvarado's; Alvarado was one of the foremost figures in his field, a respected academic, an experienced excavator and a senior government adviser on archaeological interests; and Alvarado was quite taken with the idea of stopping at least one leak in the drain of antiquities from his country. With quiet authority he motioned Richard back to his chair when he would have got up and left, and smiling gravely he examined the implications of what I had said.

Finally he asked, 'And what would you want to' – he smiled into the pause – 'borrow?'

I had given it some thought, of course, but without reaching any definite conclusion. I knew the scope of Mason's hobby, I knew what he already had – most of what he had, probably not all. There were bound to be gaps in his collection and his craving to fill them would outweigh his natural caution. But I wasn't expert enough to identify them.

'I want,' I said slowly, 'the biggest, juiciest carrot of an artifact you feel you can trust me with. It needs to be readily portable. It wants to be something whose loss would be remarked by the archaeological establishment and reported publicly. It has to be something so spectacular that there would never be another chance for him to own one. He has to know that he'll never again meet someone with access to such a thing and enough problems, or cupidity, to consider selling it.'

I avoided looking at Richard and hurried on. 'Then too, this man isn't an archaeologist himself, he's an aficionado, so it has to be something of beauty rather than purely historical importance. And if you can manage it, it wants to be something that would require careful, preferably specialised, supervision in transit.'

Three sharp glances hit me like hailstones: Cade's because I hadn't spelt that out to him, Richard's because he thought I intended roping him in even further, Alvarado's because I was asking him to entrust me not only with a national treasure but with a frail national treasure.

Ending a silence so long I thought I'd blown it, gazing up at a crystal chandelier that was absurdly ostentatious for a museum office, the Mexican said pensively, 'A Mixtec codex.'

'Jesus Christ!' swore Richard, in horror and disgust. I whispered the same words with a different intonation. Cade looked at me, his face puzzled. Alvarado was, slowly, beginning to smile again.

It was as near as damn it perfect. If Raoul Mason could pass up the chance of acquiring a codex, whatever the risks and the financial outlay, he wasn't the collector I took him for. They were rare – the expression 'hen's teeth' comes to mind, the Mixtec of southern Mexico probably created a good many of them but the Spanish priests who accompanied the Conquistadores took an obsessive dislike to native American writings and fuelled great fires with them.

They were beautiful: prepared deerhide panels decorated with pictograms describing family trees and foundation myths and the like, the colours still remarkably true after centuries. They were certainly portable, and expert supervision was indicated. The disappearance of such a thing would send shock-waves throughout meso-American archaeology, and would certainly be widely reported.

There were, among the many snags which would inevitably accompany such an undertaking, two real problems. One was that we could be overplaying the hand. It could be too tempting, too sweet a carrot. Would he suspect? Could I convince him that a treasure like that had become available, that I could get it for him, that all he had to do – besides paying me (and how much should I ask?) – was arrange to get it across the border? He knew almost nothing about me, except that my brother had died trying to crack his organisation. However much he wanted the codex, could be bring himself to trust me that far?

The other problem, of course, was the possibility that it could all go wrong and we could lose the thing.

I said, 'You want to risk that much?'

'We also stand to gain a lot,' said Alvarado.

'Where would it come from?'

'I think perhaps we should not ask Paris for theirs,' he smiled gently. 'In fact, I have a piece in mind. It is not complete but it is a good example. We are working on it now in the laboratories here. It was only discovered within the last month, we haven't announced it yet – so we can create any kind of provenance we like for it. What do you think?'

I was breathless with the possibilities, and scared to death of the responsibility. 'Are we still talking hypothetically, or are you actually offering me the loan of a new codex?'

Esteban Alvarado's gentle smile died. His eyes met mine. 'If I understand you correctly, Miss Meredith, you are offering to chance your safety in the interests of my people's history. I think we owe you the best help we can give. I'll arrange to transfer the codex to Dr Balfour. Then we'll wait to hear what you want us to do.'

The interview was over. It had been much easier, and much more profitable, than I had anticipated. There was nothing now to stop us going ahead. The realisation was terrifying.

The three of us adjourned to the canteen while Alvarado made his arrangements. That early in the day – we had taken the first available flight – most of the tables were occupied by museum staff and students, in conspiratorial knots round coffee-pots, chittering away happily and occasionally arguing in a language that seemed to bear only a passing resemblance to the Spanish I had learnt at school. But the names, of the people and the places they were talking about, were familiar.

Against that backdrop Richard began perceptibly to relax. The tension which had held him hunched in his chair in Alvarado's office leached slowly away and he gradually unwound, mentally and physically, looking both younger and taller in the process. He ordered a comprehensive, and wholly Mexican, breakfast. 'I've been on the road since three this morning,' he said, ruefully rubbing his bristles.

'I'm sorry to drag you away,' I said. 'I needed the introduction; I didn't realise Alvarado would want you to be here.'

'My time is worth nothing, except to me. He probably thought he was doing me a favour, but I hate this building. I hate everybody in it. I can't wait to get back. That god-damned jungle's killing me, but I can't give it up.' He grinned suddenly, a wolfish feral grin that split his sallow face in half. 'I guess that makes me an addict too.'

Someone called him from the door, in Spanish. He unfolded from the table and slouched away, wiping his mouth with the back of his hand, and disappeared without a word.

Cade breathed out as if he had been waiting for some time. 'Annie, I don't know how good a friend of yours he is, but that man is sick.'

I had been hoping it was just me, and the shock of seeing him again after so long. 'I know.'

'How long have you known him?'

'Since university. God, he was good then. He had the brain and he had the hands, and he had the intuition at a time when the rest of us were still groping for patterns in the dark. He was always the one who was going to do good. Mind you, nobody liked him. Even the lecturers couldn't like him. He made an art form of proving them wrong.'

The story is still told, though it may be apochryphal, about Richard Balfour and the lecturer in paleontology. It wasn't strictly relevant to our studies, but this particular speaker had got on to what was clearly a hobby-horse of his, and one of the two great mysteries in the field – the large numbers of essentially similar but still distinct species apparently co-existing in their primitive world. The other great mystery is why they all died out.

The pet theory on this occasion was sexual dimorphism. This lecturer reckoned that there were only half the number of species commonly thought: those with sails, or dorsal plates, or spiny tails were the males, and those without were the females. He projected two slides to underline the point.

Into a pause for effect, Richard had commented

laconically that the speaker had also, by his theory, solved the problem of the extinctions. 'All the males lived in Texas. All the females lived in New Mexico.'

'Lovable kind of a guy,' agreed Cade. 'But I'll tell you one thing, he hasn't got the hands now – he's got the shakes. I hope you're not planning on trusting him with much.'

I wasn't, but Alvarado was. Richard brought it back with him, rolled up in corrugated paper, sealed in a leather drum. He put it on the table between us, in a space recklessly cleared by his elbows, and first we sat and looked at the drum and then we opened it.

I had wondered at the size of the drum. The codex was even smaller. Alvarado had exaggerated when he called it incomplete: it was hardly more than a fragment, eighteen inches deep by between nine and fifteen inches wide between its ragged edges. But the size was unimportant; the fact that its sister panels had been ripped from either side, making a nonsense of the story it would once have told, seemed somehow a detail beside the towering beauty of the thing. Its beauty was more than visual, an amalgam of colour and line, though the lines were eloquently draughted and the colours rich and vibrant. It was sensual, its radiant power drawn not by the artist's hand but from his soul, passionate and consuming. I could imagine men dying for it. I could imagine men like Raoul Mason killing for it. If I could do it justice, he would take whatever risks were necessary to possess it.

After a lengthy silence Cade said, or rather whispered, 'What – exactly – is it?'

It was a piece of hide from a deer that died about the fourteenth century, surfaced with a kind of glossy distemper, covered with painted figures and symbols. What it was exactly was harder to say. The Zouche Codex is a family tree. The Fejervary-Mayer Codex is a moral homily about how the gods supervise human activities.

I looked at Richard. 'You know anything about this?'

He shrugged, like a worried stick-insect. 'I know something, but it's not my field. I can't read it. Even if there's enough of it to be read.'

'I'd better be able to tell Mason something.'

'Tell him the truth: that it's got a jaguar on it, and a headless corpse, and a couple of guys apparently trying to strangle another couple of guys, and the guy you're getting it from hasn't a notion what it means.'

'Where did it come from?'

'You don't know that,' he said sharply. 'I'm damned if we're starting a rumour that it was smuggled off any of the possible digs. It's not on, Annie. Their reputation is about the only thing most of those people have to show for decades of work, in dripping unhealthy forests and waterless bloody plains. If someone puts out a story that something has been spirited off a dig, the stigma attaches to everyone working there and it never goes away. I'm not doing that to anyone. It wouldn't matter how carefully we explained at the end, there would always be people who hadn't heard or hadn't believed the explanation. No, you tell Mason that I have it, but where I got it from is my business.'

He was right, of course, and if it was going to be a flaw in the fabric of my story it was one I was going to have to weave round. But the vehemence of his response surprised me. It wasn't just professional courtesy, it was closer to home than that. I might never know the details, certainly I would never ask, but he was speaking from experience.

It explained his obvious reluctance to be involved. His integrity had been questioned before. He must have succeeded in defending himself or he wouldn't still be working here, clearly with the ear and the confidence of the museum establishment. But if there had been questions and bitterness, however long ago, however well resolved, he could hardly welcome the opportunity to put his reputation in doubt again. I determined then that, unless my back was against the wall and I couldn't sell it any other way, I would keep his name out of my dealings with Mason.

I reckoned without that ruthless little smiler Esteban Alvarado. The news must have been on the wire as we were flying north, because it was in the evening papers that same day. Not on the front page, nor in very much detail – just one of those little News In Brief items of esoteric happenings around the world. It didn't name names either, but it was enough to cut the man's throat among his professional colleagues.

It said only that an English archaeologist had had his licence to excavate suspended by the Mexican authorities while investigations were carried out into the dis-appearance of important artifacts. Above it was a paragraph about a coco-de-mer defying horticultural precedent by thriving in a Californian monastery, and below it a story about Dobermann Pinschers eating a Jehovah's Witness.

We read it over a desultory meal in Cade's house. We were both tired – enervated, as much by the travelling as by anything we had done or were about to do. Chico had gone, leaving no message, only an unmade bed with a smear of blood on the pillow. Cade nodded at the paper. 'Do you suppose he agreed to that?'

'I dare say he did. I dare say the way they put it made it hard to say no. Do you think Mason will have seen it?'

'He'll have seen it. He's probably talked to someone in Mexico about it already. But you haven't seen it. If he refers to it you're going to be shocked and horrified, and not know whether the deal can go ahead now, and try to leave as quickly as you can. He won't let you. It'll suit him very well, knowing your source and knowing he can't afford to hang on to anything. He'll be careful, because of the investigation – he won't risk being tied into that – but he'll want to go ahead. There's no point having an advantage and not using it.'

I phoned before leaving. I kept the conversation short,

staccato, and laced with just a tempting suggestion of distress. I had to see him at once, I said. Of course: he would be at home. When could he expect me? – half an hour.

Cade took me out to my car, and stood a moment with his hand on the door before opening it. 'You can still back out, you know. You're under no obligation to put yourself at risk.'

'I want him, Josh. For what he's done to my family. This way I can have him. It's worth a risk.'

The gateman remembered me: he waved quite cheerfully as he passed me through. Then he must have called the house, because Mason was waiting on the steps when I pulled up. I grabbed my bag, with the stub of my air ticket carefully tucked into the folds of a handkerchief inside, and hurried to join him. His face was full of concern, but he said nothing as he took my elbow and steered me inside.

The hall was more fully furnished than it had been on the night of the party, forty-eight hours before. Curved sofas afforded a hedonistic view of the stele. I collapsed on to one and Mason sat down beside me, taking my hand with an almost paternal expression of anxiety. 'Angharad, whatever has happened?'

I took a deep breath. 'Raoul, I don't know what I'm doing here. I shouldn't have come. I shouldn't be involving you, of all people. But I didn't know where else … '

He touched my hand, soothing in his hand and in his voice. 'Come now, whatever you've done, it can't be that bad.'

'I haven't done anything,' I snapped back; 'at least, not yet. Oh God, I wish I hadn't gone!'

'Gone where?'

'I can't tell you!' That was what the ticket was for.

'Angharad, listen,' he said. 'You and I are very new friends, but we are friends and I want to help you. Tell me what's wrong. Even if I can't help, maybe we can hammer out a solution together. Tell me what's happened.'

So of course, since that was what I had come for, I did. I

told him I had a friend, an old friend, who worked in the
antiquities field in Mexico. When he heard I was in Texas
he invited me down south for a visit, but we were hardly
out of the airport when he broke down and started
confessing.

'He's been living high on borrowed money. God, you'd
think a European could manage on a professional salary in
a country like Mexico, wouldn't you? When the loans were
called in, the only way he could pay them off – he said –
was selling some things from the dig. Not too many,
nothing remarkable that was bound to be missed; simple
things he just never catalogued. It was too easy; he got
greedy again. People bècame suspicious.

'He has to get out, Raoul, or they'll put him in prison.
They've already got his passport. We can get him on a ship,
it we can get the money together.'

'And you want me to lend you the money?' His voice was
still gentle but there were diamonds in his eyes.

'No!' I repeated it quieter: 'No. It's not as simple as that.
He has something to sell. It's worth enough not only to get
him out of Mexico but to look after him wherever he goes.
But he has to sell it before they find it, and it has to go out
of the country. God forgive me, I thought of you.'

'What is it?' he asked.

'It's a Mixtec codex.'

It was about then that I blew my nose, leaving the
Mexico ticket to flutter under the sofa. He'd find it later,
and it would seem an unsolicited testimony.

We spent an hour poring over his books. There weren't
even many illustrations of codices, but I found one whose
colouring was comparable and another where the figures
seemed similarly engaged. Several times he said, 'You've
actually seen it?' and each time I said that I had.

'But it's not complete.'

'Oh no, far from it. But it's still a valuable prize ...' I let
my voice trail off, as if embarrassed. The 3b drama studies
group would have been proud of me.

Mason smiled. 'Indeed it is, my dear. It's also conceivable. No sane man could conceive of owning a complete codex.'

He had taken the hook.

Quite a lot later he said, 'Suppose – now, just suppose – I was to make your friend an offer for his codex. Have you thought how we'd do it?'

I worked on adoring eyes to gaze at him with. 'Oh Raoul – would you?'

'Maybe, only maybe. To help you out.' That was a lie for a start, if I'd been selling chicken shit or inflatable models of Micky Mouse he wouldn't have felt this overwhelming urge to help. 'But I have a lot to lose, I can't risk it going wrong and reflecting on me.'

'I said –' I swallowed and tried again. 'I said, if we could find a buyer, I'd act as go-between. I don't know, how are these things usually done? I could take the money down and bring back the codex.'

A polite man, he managed not to laugh in my face. 'And I would lose my money, and your friend would lose his codex, and you would lose perhaps eight years of your life. No, that would not be a sensible way to do it. Besides, until I see it how shall I know what to bid?'

'Can you go and look at it?'

He smiled. 'I could. It would be most unwise to do so.'

I could see that. 'Then what?'

'Will your friend trust you to negotiate for him?'

'Does he have a choice?'

'Then you bring me the codex, we agree a price and you return with the money.'

It wasn't much different from what I had suggested, or only in one fundamental. 'What if I get caught? I'll still lose either, or both, plus eight years of my life.'

'You won't get caught. Not if I make the arrangements.'

'That's easily said, Raoul, but – listen, don't take this wrong, but from where I'm sitting it looks as if you're happy to risk my neck doing something you wouldn't do yourself. I could spend years in a Mexican prison over this! I'm fond of my friend, I don't want to see him in trouble, but if it's a choice between him going to jail and me going for him, that's no contest. Hell, Raoul, you think maybe we should give this thing some more thought? I'm not sure either of us needs it.'

'I said, I'll make sure you don't get caught. I can arrange the whole thing, transport as well. No one that I don't trust implicitly will know about it. I promise, I can protect you.'

'Then why can't you go, and deal with – with my friend directly?'

For the first time he let the nerves show. An edge ran through his voice. 'I am not an insignificant man, Angharad. A man of substance finds it hard to move around unnoticed, even far from home. And there are other reasons.

'There is a route, and it is safe. I've used it before, when there were things I wanted to bring out of the south. You've seen some of them in this house.' He was hooked, all right. It was no longer me trying to persuade him: he was prepared to expose his flank in order to persuade me. It wasn't rational, but it showed how much he wanted the thing. He went on, talking quickly, urgently. 'Point is, it wouldn't stay safe if anyone made the connection to me. I have to use mules – couriers. Go-betweens. You said you'd do that.'

Indeed I had. There was nothing to be gained by holding out any longer, so I allowed myself to be persuaded. 'OK, Raoul, I'll do it. And – thank you.' I jutted my chin. 'I shall expect a commission.'

He laughed aloud with relief. 'Damn right you're entitled to a commission.'

'And what about some protection?'

'Protection?'

'That codex is not only valuable, it's fragile. I'm going to have my hands full looking after it. I'd feel happier if there was someone whose job it was to look after me.'

'My mules will see you come to no harm.'

'Raoul, I believe that, but look at it from my friend's point of view. He's entrusting your mules with the codex and me both, with no reason to believe he'll ever see either, or the money, again. He can't come himself, he's being watched. He just wants there to be someone there who's working for me rather than working for you. Maybe it's not necessary, but it's not unreasonable either. Is it?'

He didn't like it, but I could see him talking himself round. He was thinking of all those other people he'd shipped across the border and wondering if one more could make much difference. He knew about my brother, but knew too I had shared nothing of my brother's life. He had no reason to mistrust me, and he did want that codex. Finally I saw him decide that if my protection proved a nuisance he could always be ditched on the road. He inclined his head. 'No, that's not unreasonable.' So it was decided.

'When should I go?'

'Tomorrow. The less delay the better. You and Savannah will fly down, ostensibly to see the sights of Mexico City. My daughter will undoubtedly see much of interest, but you will meet your friend, collect his package – and your bodyguard – and rendezvous with my mule. The round trip back to Mexico City will take a couple of days. Then you give your friend his money, pick up Savannah and fly home. What could be more innocent than a couple of girls spending a few days in a glamorous city? People round here do it all the time.'

I stood up. 'Raoul, I'm very grateful. You showed me kindness and friendship before this came up, now you're going out on a limb to help me. I shan't forget that. I'm only glad I have something worthwhile to offer in return. You won't be disappointed, I promise.'

He smiled broadly. He was a devastatingly handsome man. 'A Mixtec codex? No, I don't think I'll be disappointed.'

I offered my hand. 'Well, I'd better get back to my motel and pack.'

He took it, but only to steer me towards the stairs. 'Give Savannah your key, she'll get your things. I know you'll forgive me, but we've talked of sensitive matters tonight. By the time you bring the codex here I shall have papers for it which will defy expert scrutiny, but until then I shall sleep happier with you under my roof.'

It was a wise precaution for the man to take, and if I hadn't been trying to rip him off it could have raised no obstacle to my plans. I had to smile and accept it.

Before we went to bed we sent a wire to Richard to expect me, and I hoped he'd have the wit to pass it on to Cade.

3

The next morning I was back on an aeroplane heading for Mexico. I was clearly remembered at the airport because I was subjected to much more than casual inquiry and inspection. But there was nothing for them to find and so they passed me through. I was deeply glad our plan had not involved me in smuggling contraband through there: I don't know where I'd have had to put it to escape detection.

I wasn't sure how much Savannah knew. Obviously her father had briefed her on her role, because she knew what was expected of her and she knew better than to chatter about it on the plane. Whether she was aware of what I would be doing while she was seeing the sights of Mexico City on her own, I couldn't tell. She must have known that our activities were illicit: I wondered if she also knew that, as well as smuggling antiquities for pleasure, her father also smuggled immigrants and drugs for profit, and sometimes he killed people.

We went into the city and checked into our hotel, and

followed our bags up to our rooms; and immediately I
went out again, alone, and made my way to the Zócalo, and
stood under the colonnade of the Palacio del Ayun-
tamiento, which is one hell of a name for a city hall, and
admired the spectacular architecture of the great square
for twenty minutes until Richard picked me up in a jeep.

He drove fast, dodging pedestrians and bicycles. The
frantic rattle of the elderly vehicle and the flapping of its
imperfectly secured soft-top made conversation impossible. It was also unnecessary. His face, caught in angular
profile against the racing, lurching buildings, was dark
with anger and something like despair.

We shed the city in bursts of speed up good roads, and
somewhere east of the airport he turned south, making a
couple of junctions more by inches than seconds, then
drove between trees and stopped with his foot hard on the
brake. The old jeep nodded its bonnet in surprise, fell
silent as he killed the engine with a savage flick of the wrist.

Before us the sky hung bright blue and empty, impaled
improbably on two snow-clad peaks: the twin volcanoes of
Iztaccihuatl and Popocatépetl. The snowline ran along the
ridge dividing them, making a false horizon. Below the
snow the hills were the colour of blue-john, fading
gradually to green in the valley. The spring had already
begun here, the sun pouring through the sharp clear air.
Mexico City is a child of the mountains, and nowhere is the
relationship clearer than gazing up the high valley towards
the old twin sisters in their lace mantillas.

I got as far as, 'Richard –'

The anger, the bitterness, the sense of betrayal burst
from him in a cataract. 'You damned interfering little cow!
Do you know what you've done to me? – you and that
devious scheming bastard Alvarado? My God, you don't –
of course you don't, why would you, but he knows. He
knew what he was doing when he set this up. He knew
what he was doing to me.'

'Richard, I don't –'

'Understand? No. What do you know about museum politics? – you with your safe little schoolmarm job in safe little Wales. What do you know about Mexico? You spend ten years of your life in a god-damned rain forest, breaking your back and poisoning your blood, piecing together their history for a bunch of people who hadn't the gumption to keep it together when they had it, and it's smiles and gratitude all round for the clever foreign doctor, and they'd probably give him some money to work with as well if they weren't so bloody gormless with their finances that it takes more pesos to buy a roll of wallpaper than it takes to cover the god-damned wall!'

His hands, long and strong and grained with ten years of jungle humus, vigorous with his fury so the tremor didn't show, fed him a thin tarry cheroot from the breast pocket of his shirt, and lit it, and failed to return to any kind of rest, drumming feverishly on the big steering-wheel. The smell of the cheroot was pungent in my nostrils. I had not remembered him smoking but, judging from the urgent, hungry way he sucked the smoke deep into his lungs, it was not a new habit.

'And then one day there's an accident, and people get killed because the safety equipment they've given you has already been thrown out by the mining department; and with the world's press looking on they need a scapegoat, and all the other candidates are local boys and the real culprit is a minister's nephew when he's not pretending to work for the safety inspectorate. And you don't hear so much then about the clever foreign doctor, just this irresponsible alien exploiter who's caused the deaths of good Mexican workers, and maybe it's true what they say about him using money allocated for safety to line his own pocket.'

He didn't so much stop as run out of words. I ached with regret. 'Richard, I'm so sorry.'

'It wasn't true. Alvarado knew it wasn't true. He knew what the allocation was, and how hard it was even to get what we were promised, and how many miracles we performed just to keep digging. I owe him this much: they wanted me hung out to dry and he wouldn't have it. I could have gone to prison. Well, he saved me from that, but I've lived in his pocket ever since. I've paid him back a dozen times. He didn't have to do this to me.'

'Richard, I don't know what to say. I didn't know any of this.'

'Of course you didn't. Why would you? But he knew. He knew to the last syllable how little he had to say and still let everyone know who the – the thief was.' Even saying it cost him. 'If your friend Mason has contacts down here, however casual, and they know anything about antiquities, they're going to know who's supposed to have stolen that codex. And they're going to remember, and so is everyone else, long after Mason's gone to prison and you've gone home.

'You know enough about excavating to know how much of it is founded on trust. I'm never going to be trusted again, here or anywhere else. If I work it'll be on sufferance, under Alvarado's protection, and with someone always looking over my shoulder. If I want anything better than that I'm going to have to find myself another continent, where the archaeologists don't read the trade press.'

He seemed finally to have finished, the anger and the grief more exhausted than expiated. He hunched, string thin, like an undernourished vulture, over the steering-wheel, his hands clenched on it like talons, still that faint tremor visible along the backs of his knuckles.

I was deeply sorry for him, felt for his hurting. But he was holding me responsible for everything that had gone wrong in his life, and I had neither the time nor the energy to carry his problems as well as my own. A certain tartness crept into my voice, and I didn't make too much effort to disguise it.

'All right, Richard. I've drawn you into something you'd

rather have stayed clear of. I'm sorry about that, I wish it could have been avoided. But it will all be over in three or four days, the ungodly will be behind bars, the codex will be back in the museum and the tabloids will be singing the praises of all who devised, authorised and took part in so bold and successful an enterprise. I know enough of museum politics to know the publicity that will generate for your work, and that money always follows where publicity has led. Yes, it's a risk, something could go wrong and leave you with egg on your face. But at least you stand to gain more than you stand to lose, which is more than can be said for anyone else involved, including me.'

'You chose to be included. I didn't.'

'Well perhaps you should have. Perhaps I shouldn't have to be sitting here explaining to you that the issues at stake are more important than a bit of tarnish on your reputation.'

'To you!'

'Certainly to me: my life is one of them. My brother's life has already been forfeit. You probably consider that was his choice too, and you're right. He went into it with his eyes wide open; but I don't suppose that stopped him being shit-scared all the time, and hurting like hell when they killed him.'

We were both angry now, both saying things we would later wish unsaid.

'Goes with the territory,' snarled Richard. 'Archaeologists get dirty, teachers get smart, Feds get killed. Life goes on.'

I think if there had been more room in the jeep I would have struck him. As it was I gaped, literally open-mouthed, at his callousness, his selfish cynicism. Even when I found my voice I had to wait, because all my instincts were to scream. Finally I managed a kind of controlled hiss.

'You arrogant bastard! Oh, you arrogant bloody man. All right. You don't care about Cristóbal and the six men who died with him. You don't care about the Mexicans cheated and exploited every day by men like Mason who promise them the world and pull the plug on them at the first sign of a problem. You don't care about the American kids rotting slowly on drugs smuggled over the Mexican border. OK: you want to opt out of the human race, that's your business.

'But don't you feed me the outraged professional line, because also going across that border are some of this country's historical treasures, and if it's not your job to stop that I don't know who the hell's job it is. Well, this time I'm going to do it for you, with your approval or without it, and if it's inconvenient for you I'm sorry but it's the only time and the only place I can do it.

'But afterwards, when it's all over and we're all congratulating ourselves round a bottle of tequila, you'd better spend some time wondering if there's anything you care enough about to take a stand on. Because if there isn't, it's not a new continent you need, it's a new planet – one with no other people on it.'

The codex in its leather drum was on the seat behind us. I twisted round in my seat and reached for it. Richard twisted in his and slapped my hand away. We glared at one another, nose to nose.

'Do I have to remind you that your principal authorised this thing?'

'Do I have to remind you that my principal made me responsible for that thing?'

'So what do you want to do? – take it on a scenic tour of the city and then drive it home?'

At about the same time we became aware of the Mexican kid watching us through the windscreen. He had wandered up through the scrub while we were arguing, and found himelf a comfortable spot beneath one of the shock-haired trees and hunkered down against the gnarled and figured bark. He was regarding us now with frank if undemonstrative interest. There was no one in sight except we three.

I asked Richard, 'Are you expecting someone?'

'Yes.' He got out of the jeep, leaving the codex on the back seat. After a moment I got out too. The kid stood up, in an easy movement that suggested he spent more time sitting on floors than in chairs.

He was older than I had thought – the brash, self-sufficient swagger that teenagers work so hard on had already diminished to a mere self-possession in the way he held himself that said he had reached the real independence of not caring what impression he made – but still young enough to be wearing up his universal youth uniform of jeans and a denim jacket over an open-necked shirt. His grandfather's poncho would have kept him warmer in the thin mountain air, which had more spring in it than heat, but he would as soon have worn the old man's sombrero.

Without moving away from the jeep Richard shouted, 'Who sent you?'

The boy nodded his head at me. 'She knows.'

For a moment I didn't. There seemed nothing familiar about him, not the face, not even the voice: one Mexican in a city of fifteen million in a country of sixty million more. I started to say, 'No I don't,' and he started to smile, sardonically, and only then did I recognise him. 'Chico?'

You couldn't honestly call it a disguise, more that he had shrugged off one national persona and slipped quite subtly into another. Certainly he had darkened his hair and his skin, rubbing in something that had both deepened the colour and masked those bruises his clothes didn't cover. When you looked you knew he had been fighting, but you wouldn't have said it was within the last week.

But the stain, useful enough in that context. was somehow the least of it. You could have fitted Richard out in a Kentucky minstrel outfit and he'd still and always have been a white English academic, instantly recognisable as such. What Chico had was a happy knack of blending into his background. In Texas he was a cowboy, in Sugar Valley he was a thief, down here he was a Mexican, and I didn't' doubt that if the job ever required his attendance in Washington DC he'd don a suit and start tapping his Rolex with the best of them. Protective coloration: the art of not standing out in a crowd. He probably owed his life to it: and probably, one day, it would get him killed.

I said, weakly and not it seemed for the first time, 'I don't understand.'

Chico flicked me his grin and turned away, looking up the valley to the two old ladies white-haired against the sky. Always he seemed to seek sanctuary in distance.

Richard answered. He sounded bewildered, as if I should have known, and perhaps I should. 'Your wire. I called your friend from Border Patrol, told him it was going down and when. He said fine, he had a minder laid on and we arranged to meet him here.'

'You, Chico? You're crazy!' He was crazy, and Cade was even crazier. He had helped me build a maze around the minotaur, then provided me with a Theseus I didn't dare use. After all my plotting and persuasion it was going to be me alone in there with my little ball of string, the codex under one arm and nothing but enemies all round. Cade had wanted me to take a companion, and the fact that Mason had agreed perhaps suggested I didn't need one, but it had been like a weight lifted from my shoulders. Now the weight was back, crushing, dropped on me from a great height, and fear and loneliness surged in me like a tide. Literally reeling with shock, I leaned on the bonnet of the jeep for support.

Richard looked at me with something akin to concern. 'What's the matter?'

'Him!' I cried. 'I come here to meet a bodyguard and I find him?'

He looked at Chico curiously. 'What's wrong with him?'

'Mason knows him, that's all!'

Chico turned back, very fast, his face hard, his eyes

sparking like coals. 'Oh no he don't,' he said with absolute conviction.

'Chico, I *saw* you there. Three nights ago. His people were beating the crap out of you. Remember?'

He shook his head. Behind the bruises and the stain there was an intensity in his face which I could not then fathom. 'Raoul Mason has never set eyes on me. He has no reason to believe I exist.'

'And those men at the gate?'

'Might recognise me again and might not. It was dark, and they were pretty busy at the time. Besides, it was no big thing to them – they were just doing their job, keeping out thieves. I doubt they'd recognise me if we met face to face in broad daylight.'

'You *doubt*? Chico, you may be willing to risk your life on the balance of probabilities – '

'Will you listen when I'm talking to you?' he snapped back, angrily, as though I were a child and not a woman more than ten years his senior. 'It doesn't matter if they have photographic memories. They mind the gate at Sugar Valley. You think Mason's going to suddenly switch them to his smuggling operation? I mean, when he's got something coming up he cares about strongly and personally, he really needs three gatemen running the job, yes? The only place we're going to see them again is where we saw them before, and if we get that far it won't matter a damn who recognises who because we'll have the Seventh Cavalry right behind us, and Josh Cade is going to hand me my authority just in time for me to arrest Mason personally.'

What he said made sense, but the panic was rising in me, more pressing and more real than words, mainly because I had succeeded in suppressing it till now. I had got this far on a cocktail of anger, vengeance and ego, with a good measure of convenient (rather than happy) coincidence stirred in, the whole laced with that heady surrealism you get from travelling far from home. I wouldn't have been

doing this in Swansea; I wouldn't even have been doing it
in London. The realisation of what I had begun and its
implications, for all of us but mostly for me, had finally hit
me like a sledgehammer. I whispered, '*If* we get that far?'

All the stridency dropped from his voice. The man was a
chameleon: physically, vocally, emotionally. He spoke
gently, with that strange innocence in his eyes that had
surprised me back at the motel. 'It's all right to be afraid.'

I looked up at him, moved almost to tears by his
kindness as I had never been by his jibes. For the first time
clearly I saw the strength in him that enabled him to do
this; and to do it not once, like me, but again and again,
knowing that even as his skill increased, so inevitably did
the odds on him or someone making the mistake that
would bury him.

Me cracking up on him could make that lethal
difference this time. He knew that. To varying degrees he
had been trusting me with his life since that first decision
to compromise his cover in order to tell me about
Cristóbal. He knew the risk and had come ready to take it,
and if I could pull myself together he would go through
with it. He left me with no option but to do the same.

He was right. I was entitled to be afraid – it would be
absurd not to be, I could get seriously hurt doing this – but
I was committed. There was no way back that didn't
involve total abdication, not fear but cowardice. He'd
judged I wouldn't go that far, and he was right there too;
but only just. I raked up a feeble grin. 'I didn't expect to
be.'

He smiled. 'It's the fear that keeps you alive.'

Belatedly I introduced them, the English archaeologist
and the American agent, adding for Richard's benefit a
potted version of my earlier encounters with Chico. By this
time we were all back in the jeep, with Richard driving and
Chico in the back, eyeing the leather drum as if he
wondered what a codex was.

4

Such as they were, I had the instructions for contacting our courier. Raoul Mason had given them to me that morning as he had driven Savannah and me to the airfield. Even at the time they seemed a bit scanty.

'There's a place called San Mateo Atitzayanca, about seventy miles east of the city. My man will meet you there.'

'When?'

'When you get there.'

'How shall I know him?'

'He'll know you.'

I'd spent most of the flight repeating the name to myself. The steward thought I was muttering some kind of paternoster, told me how safe flying was and plied me with drinks I didn't need at that hour of the morning.

Chico had never been there, but Richard had and chuckled darkly at the prospect of going again. 'Well, it explains one thing – how you'll know the man you're supposed to meet.'

'How?'

'He'll be the one who's there when we arrive.'

For most of an hour we drove over roads that were surprisingly good, heading always east, while the temperature mounted steadily towards a pleasant midday. Once we stopped to drop the soft-top in an untidy heap in the back of the jeep. At a small town with a name like a sneeze we turned north, on what the map described endearingly as a road 'practicable all the year round'. After it crossed the railway line, however, our map admitted it was no more than a track. It was the sort of country where Joshua Cade's uncle would have made a fortune. I began to understand Richard's cryptic references to San Mateo.

But we never got there. In the middle of nowhere, on a track in imminent danger of turning into a path, we were flagged down by a farmer, standing by the rear wheel of a flatbed truck piled four-deep with crates of live poultry. Where he could be taking so many birds on so poor a road I could not imagine, but I thought he was a farmer and his truck had broken down.

Richard stopped the jeep and addressed the man in Spanish. He responded in English. 'You are going to San Mateo Atitzayanca?' he asked me.

There aren't too many places in the world where a woman travelling with two men will be asked their plans by a third man none of them knows. Wales isn't one, and I felt sure Mexico wasn't another. The farmer was waiting for us, knew who we were.

I said, 'Not any more, I would guess.'

He grinned at that, a big grin full of broken teeth stained with tobacco juice. 'Maybe you like a drive round the countryside instead.'

'I think we'd like that very much.'

Richard said, 'I'm coming too.'

I don't know which of us was most stunned, me or Chico or Richard himself. Only the farmer remained sanguine, blithely unaware of the drama unfolding quietly before him. 'That's OK, I got room for two.'

Chico whispered viciously behind us, 'What the hell is he talking about?'

I took a deep breath, fighting for calm. 'Richard, you know Chico's coming with me. That's what we arranged.'

'Then we'll all go.'

The farmer looked at me just that shade more sharply than a farmer would. 'Two. They told me to bring two.'

I nodded encouragement. 'Yes, two. That's right.'

'Well, I'm being one of them.' Before either of us thought to stop him Richard had twisted round and snatched the leather drum off the back seat. 'Either I go north with it, or this stays here.'

A surge of helplessness washed up through me, followed by another of frustration. 'Richard, I don't understand.'

'Exactly. You don't understand.' That desperate, bitter anger was running like a tide in him again. 'You have no conception of just how valuable this thing is. I'm not letting it out of my sight.'

'You don't trust me with it?'

'You're damn right I don't trust you with it! And as for him,' he added, jerking his head at Chico, 'what the hell do I know about him?'

There was desperation in my voice too, I could hear it myself as I struggled to draw him away from the abyss he seemed determined to kick us all into. 'You know what we agreed. It was all decided: Chico and I go north, and I' – this for the farmer's benefit – 'I'll bring the money back. That's what we agreed. You have to stay here or you'll be missed. You're the one who needs the alibi.' It wasn't the best cover story anyone ever came up with, but it explained why Richard had to stay and therefore why Chico had to come, which was what had to happen.

'I'm not worried about the money.' Well, of course he wouldn't be. 'I'm worried about this.' He held it in front of him, covetously, like a favourite teddy. 'I don't think either of you knows what we've really got here. If anything were to happen to it – '

'Richard, I know exactly what we've got there. I'm an historian too, remember? What we have there' – oh, how I wished we could have had this argument earlier, alone, not under the eyes and ears of the organisation we were out to break! – 'is the money you need to get safely out of this country, and if you can't get a grip on yourself and behave normally for the next couple of days it isn't going to matter how much money it fetches, you're not going to be in a position to spend it.'

I wasn't getting through to him at all. He was too angry, too upset, maybe too hurt to give a toss for what had been decided without his vote or agreed to without his consent.

He was oblivious of the danger, the real immediate danger he was exposing all three of us to. The only thing he cared about was that fragment of painted deerhide curled up in its leather cocoon. He wasn't going to give it up.

He wasn't even going to be discreet about it. 'Screw the money. You can't buy a thing like this. And screw you for –'

The movement behind me caught my eye, and the brief glimpse of the gun in Chico's hand made me cry out. I hadn't known he had it, and for a moment I thought he intended to shoot this half-demented man clutching his treasure to his chest.

But it wasn't murder he had in mind, just self-preservation. The infinitely intricate piece of weaponry, acting for once with the same ballistic complexity as half a brick, caught Richard behind the ear, cutting him off midway through that lethal sentence. He grunted and his face folded up with the shock of an assault his consciousness lasted barely long enough to register; then his long figure went slack and he slumped sideways into my lap, and the codex tumbled to the floor of the jeep at my feet.

Chico vaulted over the side of the vehicle, the gun already back in his pocket or wherever he had brought it from. His hand touched my arm. 'Time to go.'

I stared at him, open-mouthed. 'We can't leave him – here, like this – '

'Five minutes from now he'll start coming round. In half an hour he'll be able to drive himself back to the city. He'll be OK.'

'You had no right – !'

His eyes gazed into mine from a range of inches, very directly, and they were darker than I remembered. The almost accentless voice he reserved for me was quiet and deliberate. 'Annie, he was going to get us all killed. Now if you're coming, come on.'

I couldn't get out for Richard's body across my knees. I tried to lift him carefully and couldn't. Chico lifted him off me by the simple expedient of a handful of hair, and let him slump back across the seat when I was out. He passed me the drum. 'Don't forget this.'

The farmer introduced himself, improbably, as Freddy. Looking back at the jeep he said, 'The man said to bring two. You better be the right two.'

I looked at Chico, then flicked him a brief smile. 'We're the right two.'

Chico helped me up into the high cab and passed me the codex. He was swinging up behind me when something happened which I couldn't see but which made him catch his breath and pause for a moment, suspended between the cab and the ground with one foot in midair. Then he lowered himself carefully to the ground again. Then I could see what the problem was. The bucolic Freddy had a gun of his own, pressed to the small of Chico's back.

With a faint note of apology in his voice he said, 'The man said, no guns except this one.'

'I'm supposed to be her bodyguard!'

Freddy appeared to consider this for a moment. 'You should take up kung fu.'

I had no idea how Chico would react, or if he had expected this. My stomach tied itself in granny knots while I waited to see. Slowly he began to chuckle, and reached carefully and awkwardly across his body to draw the weapon with the fingertips of his left hand. Passing it over he said, 'I reckon you'd cut my hands off.'

The Mexican grinned back. 'It's supposed to be unarmed combat.' They laughed together like friends while my insides ached, then Chico climbed up on one side of me and Freddy walked round the bonnet and climbed up on the other.

He had one more trick up his unsophisticated peasant sleeve. 'Put these on.'

They were wrap-around sunglasses with dark, slightly mirrored glass, of a pattern usually associated with gold medallions and designer stubble. He handed us a pair each. When we put them on I found that the glass was opaque. Apparently hitch-hiking, effectively blindfolded, we were driven into the darkness of a sunny Mexican afternoon, with the cab radio blaring out to make sure we were deaf as well as blind.

At first I tried to keep some sort of mental record of distance and direction, but the longer we travelled over those rough and featureless roads the more difficult it became, until in the end I didn't know if we were heading north or south and lost track of the time as well.

We didn't talk: even had we been of a mind for conversation, the Tijuana brass trumping out of Freddy's radio would have made it all but impossible. A couple of times the truck stopped and shook gently, the engine turning over, and then moved off again in a manner that suggested other traffic. Once we ran for a time on a made-up road before leaving it again for an earth track. Once we waited for a longer time that ended with a rumbling vibration, heard above the radio and felt through the turning of the engine, that had to be a train. Then we went on again.

Finally we stopped, and the engine stopped, and Freddy leaned over my knees to turn the bloody radio off. 'You can take the shades off now.'

The light was shocking and the silence rang. The solar glare was reflected everywhere, bleaching away the colours. I winced and screwed up my eyes.

A voice I didn't know said, 'You can get down now, Miss Meredith,' and a hand came to guide me.

As my eyes adjusted to the light I saw that the truck had come into a yard. Whitewashed walls on three sides bounced the sun around like a ball before throwing it at me. On the fourth side, behind us, was a shorter wall and a big iron gate. If it wasn't designed as a prison it could easily have served as one.

The man helping me down was an American, a tall well-made individual in his mid-thirties with sandy hair and unusually light blue eyes. It was as if the Mexican sun had washed the colour out of them too. His voice was low, with a modulation that spoke of both education and intelligence, and an accent that was midwest rather than specifically Texas. Freddy was local labour, but this man was undoubtedly Mason's.

I screwed my eyes up and cranked my head back to look at him. 'You are – ?'

'Blair.' There was only the briefest pause to show he had wondered whether to answer. It didn't, of course, tell me whether his answer was the truth. 'Is that the merchandise?'

I was still hugging the drum to my frontage. 'Yes.'

'I was told to take a look at it.'

I looked round. A catchy little wind was flicking the dust round the yard. 'Not out here. I don't want any dirt getting in. If you know what this is, you know how fragile it is, and how valuable.'

'We'll go inside.'

There were a number of doors in the walls round us. Blair led the way to one of them, standing back at the last moment to let me precede him. It might have been good manners that he got the same place he got his way of speaking, but in fact it was so he could stop Chico from following us. 'Don't need you just now, boy.'

Chico smiled at him quite amiably but neither backed off nor turned away. 'Where she goes, I go. That's my job.'

Blair raised an eyebrow in my direction. 'Miss Meredith?'

I shrugged, half apologetically. 'It was agreed I could bring him. As a bodyguard. Well, mainly to guard this.' There was a plain deal table in the small room and I put the leather drum on it.

'I see.' After a moment longer he came inside, leaving the door open. Chico stepped just inside the room and stayed there. Blair didn't look at him.

I opened the drum and carefully unpacked the codex.

In that tiny, dirty room, lit only by the sunlight through the door, spread out on a plain board table, it glowed – with life and colour and the sun of lost centuries. I heard, Blair catch his breath. The potency of the thing was remarkable. No wonder Mason wanted it, and Richard didn't want to risk it.

I followed up the advantage. 'You see? That's what it's all about. That's why it's worth men's fortunes, and careers, and consciences. It's been in this world for six hundred years. It was already old when King James authorised an English-language bible, and when Shakespeare sharpened his first pencil, and when the Old Masters were still painting by numbers. That, and the city where it was made, and the civilisation which spawned it, were raised out of the jungle by a people with an almost cosmic concept of time and scale at a period when your ancestors all belonged to someone else, carried garlic to ward off the evil eye and believed menstruating women turned the milk sour. What I'm saying to you, Mr Blair, is that this is very, very precious.'

'I hear you.' The words came from a distance.

'Which is why we shall not be fording any streams with it, screwing it for safe keeping behind the spare wheel, or wearing it under our vests in an attempt to smuggle it unnoticed through customs. Before I will do any of those things I will surrender it, because I will not be responsible for its destruction, and it would be as easy to destroy as the pattern on a butterfly's wing. Outside the closely monitored conditions of a museum laboratory, in fact, the difficulty is going to be keeping it intact.

'Well, I can do it, given your co-operation and just a little bit of luck, but I want to be quite sure that *you* know that the man paying both of us is not going to be pleased if anything happens which prevents me from doing it. That's why I need a bodyguard, why Mason agreed to me having a bodyguard, and why you too need me to have a bodyguard. Yes?'

In the close darkness of the misty little room Blair looked at me, and turning slowly looked at Chico, and looked lingeringly at the unrolled codex that was a patch of glory on the table. Then he smiled thinly.

'Miss Meredith, I intend to get that – thing – to the man who's picking up the tab because that is my job; and since that means getting you there too, I guess I can take a bit of crap from you. But I don't have to take any crap from him, because all the protection you need you'll get from me, as part of the package. So keep the greaser out of my light, or I'll break his back.'

He was still smiling, and he nodded to Chico as he passed him in the door. 'Get that thing packed away, we're moving out.'

5

When he had gone I found my hands were shaking too much to handle the codex. I had visions of it dissolving in a snowstorm of chalky flakes. Chico packed it for me, with care but no reverence. His hands were steady. 'Just in case you're wondering,' he murmured as he worked, 'it is far too late to turn back now.'

I managed a shaky grin. 'If I get killed doing this, my little brother is *never* going to hear the end of it.'

He passed me the drum but didn't turn away when I took it. 'Is that what this is all about?'

'Cristóbal? Of course. Or at least, as far as I'm concerned.' I didn't understand the question. He knew why I was here. Did he imagine I had some other motive? I was risking my life and I was frightened out of my wits: did he still think it was some kind of ego trip? Well, maybe it was. There's no seasoning, no spice, no aphrodisiac like vengeance.

He still couldn't leave it alone. 'But you didn't know him.'

'I didn't have to. He's in my blood. We Celts go a whole bundle on blood, you know. Read Dylan Thomas sometime.'

He had. He was a most surprising cowboy. His quote was not only accurate but apt. 'Do not go gentle into that good night: rage, rage against the dying of the light.'

We exchanged a smile, our first gesture of mutual respect, and walked out into the yard, and Chico went back to being a Mexican minder.

Freddy and his poultry were gone. A rumble beyond the open gate heralded the arrival of fresh horses.

We use the word Juggernaut too loosely at home. We tend to apply it to anything with more wheels than corners, that can't do a 360 at a pimple roundabout without shuffling. That is a lorry. It may even be a big lorry, and leave cracked kerb-stones and shaky foundations in its wake if cutbacks in the bypass programme compel it to drive through little mediaeval towns with quaint names and half-timbering. But a juggernaut is something else, and I doubt anyone appreciates that whose driving experience has been limited to the UK. Even European transporters built up to the full EEC specification are barely juggernauts.

This was a juggernaut. Its cab reared as high as a single-storey house. It was as wide as a train. Silver smoke-stacks decorated the skyline. It was so long it couldn't get into the yard: when the front of the cab was eyeball to eyeball with the far wall, the second trailer was still mostly outside. There were two trailers, each the length of a railway carriage.

Blair was watching my face with some amusement. 'You reckon you're going to have enough room?'

'Me, and half the population of the Gower Peninsula.'

He didn't know what that meant, but he got the idea and grinned.

'How many of us are travelling?'

He looked along the steel and timber wagons that

loomed over us like a cliff. 'You and the greaser. Forty wets. A small quantity of other commodities. And forty tons of cotton.'

'You smuggle cotton?'

'No, cotton smuggles us.' Enjoying my confusion, he walked away.

Chico understood. 'Cotton is one of Mexico's exports. Trucks like this cross the border all the time. The manifest will be for forty-five tons, the actual load forty tons, there'll be room for us inside and some heavy ballast to make up the difference so the weighbridge gives the right reading. People don't weigh enough for the space they take up.'

'And the other commodities?'

'Drugs, most likely. They don't weigh much either, but they don't need space to breathe. I hope you don't get claustrophobic.'

'Why?'

Blair had gone round to the far side of the rig. Through the gap between tractor and trailer I saw him unlock – not just open but unlock – the door set into the opposite wall. The room must have been larger than the one we had used, at least I hope so, because when he flung the door wide a lot of people came out.

With all the brake-lines and electrical gear between us, most of what I could see was legs: legs in jeans and in cotton trousers, and in calf-length cotton skirts, feet in boots and espadrilles and sandals, and some proud and awkward in best shoes that clearly weren't going to last the course.

They came slowly, hesitantly, as if they didn't trust their eyes to guide them, as if their eyes were blind from being locked in the dark. I heard Blair shouting to hurry them up, and caught glimpses of his big frame, purposeful against the colourful disorder around him, directing their tentative and uncertain movements, imposing organisation on the fundaments of chaos. He seemed to be dividing them into two groups, sending one to the forward trailer and one to the after. It might have been a school outing, viewed through the steel and cable screen, but for the near absence of sound.

They didn't move in silence, of course, these people who were buying the chance to slip as fugitives out of their native land, but their voices were kept low, uncertain as their steps, without laughter or curiosity or complaint. There was something immensely sad about their quiet obedience, sad and not far from sinister.

Two men had dropped down from the cab. They split up too, one going to the front of each trailer. They dropped on their hands and knees and crawled underneath, and neither reappeared.

'Because,' said Chico, answering my forgotten query, 'that's the way in.'

We moved closer and hunched down to watch. The first of the best shoes met their Waterloo there and then: high heels snapped, and it seemed to me a minor miracle that no ankles did likewise, as their owners crawled under the trailers, rolled on to their backs, then kicked and clawed their way up into a space between the floorboards. We could see the hands of the crewmen coming down to guide and help them.

About the time the third three-inch stiletto went springing gaily across the yard, the waiting women quietly put down their rolls – each had just as many belongings as she could carry under her arm – and removed their own best shoes, and waited barefoot for their turn.

Even when their shoes didn't break, they got oil on their clothes and dirt in their hair, and skinned their knees in the graceless commando sprawl, and broke their fingernails and spilt their chattels in the dust. Still no one complained; only once did I hear someone sob. It was as if they had pawned whatever rights and dignities they possessed to buy this grim leaving and the unknowable exile that awaited them. I hoped to God it was going to be worth it to them. I wondered what unutterable misery they were escaping that made them accept such treatment. It was easier for the men, of course, though perhaps only physically. Emotionally it may have been harder.

When they had all disappeared into the bowels of the vehicle, all the anxious quiet people in their spoilt best clothes, the driver emerged from under the second trailer and stood up, dusting himself down. Blair came round the front. 'You two travel in the first trailer.'

Not until that moment had I realised I would be expected to subject myself to the same undignified scramble and endure the same squalid concentration between the cotton bales as those other criminals. My pity had gone out to them, but I had not expected to share their plight. I don't quite know what I had expected instead.

'You want us to ride in there?' I stammered, aware as I said it that the cynical humour in Blair's face would be matched by something even less flattering in Chico's behind me.

'That was the general idea.'

I was embarrassed enough to stumble on. 'I thought, maybe there'd be room in the cab – ?'

Blair, demonstrating that special patience we reserve for idiots and children, only rolled his eyes a little. 'Lady, I don't know how to say this without being rude, but you are not the colour or stamp of the women who travel these roads in trucks, and you are not the age of a woman in whom it would seem just a youthful eccentricity. You are, and you'll forgive me for saying this, just too old and too white to be riding shotgun.'

The snort of mirth behind me was wholly unsympathetic. I fled it without turning, and scrambled under the vehicle like John Wayne in his *Green Beret* days, and needed hardly any help to haul myself up inside the trailer, such was my haste to escape into the dark. A moment later Chico squirmed in behind me, and the bastard was still chuckling.

It wasn't dark inside, just dark enough that our eyes –
which had been swinging from bright sun to nearly none
all day – had to spend time adjusting once more. The light
came in between the bales, mostly from above, through
narrow gaps left by accident or design during the stacking.
The bales above us were carried on wooden slats at head
height. I could stand upright. Chico could stand upright
with his hair brushing the slats. Anyone taller would have
been obliged to duck.

The gallery between the bales was wide enough for two
people to sit facing one another, as long as they knew one
another quite well, and for a third to squeeze sideways
between their knees. The lowest tier of bales on each side
projected to form seating most of the length of the trailer.
At a pinch the gallery would have taken more than the
twenty-two people there, so we arranged ourselves in a
herringbone pattern, with a little extra space for our
elbows and to stretch our legs. Under our feet were
concrete blocks, the ballast to make the weight right.

When we were all in place, our crewman said, 'We're
going to be travelling about five hours. We won't stop in
that time unless we're stopped: if that happens everybody
keeps quiet. Nobody smokes; nobody so much as lights a
match. If anybody can't wait till we stop, there's a bucket
back there. If anybody starts fretting to get out, his friends
better sit on him because this' – he indicated the hatch
behind him – 'is the only way, and the only time we ever
had someone open it from inside he was fifteen different
kinds of dead by the time the wheels stopped rolling over
him. Don't worry about the air getting in: since there ain't
enough room for square-dancing and any singing's just
liable to give us all away, you'll have enough.'

That was it. He dropped down through the hatch and a
moment later we heard the clips screwing it in place. There
was a minute's uneasy waiting – now we could see one
another inside the dim space we avoided each other's eyes
except for the occasional quick smile, given and received as

an almost embarrassing intimacy – and then the big diesel started up again, sending a tremor the length of the rig, and we jerked and jolted backwards out of the yard. When that stopped we felt the gear-change and the building surge of power come at us through the floor, and then we were on our way.

I waited for Chico's eyes, moving purposefully round the gallery, taking in the faces of the twenty people who were offenders and victims in the same crime, to come to me. When they did I cast him a grin that was at once apology and forgiveness, and said, 'Here's another fine mess you've gotten me into.'

Someone giggled. Being handled like cattle, even at one's own behest, does little for the sense of humour and it was probably the first joke anyone had made for a while. The quality hardly mattered. I looked round, interested and somehow reassured to learn that there were other English speakers and at least one other Laurel & Hardy fan on board.

The giggle had come, and in a somewhat muffled form was still coming, from my neighbour-but-one on the right-hand side, towards the rear of the trailer. She was about nineteen, quite tall but very slender, long legs encased in tight jeans and long arms in a bright print shirt. She had a knitted jacket across her knees and high-heeled leather boots under the turned-up cuffs of her jeans. Her short black hair was restrained by a colourful headband. Her eyes were bright with laughter, her teeth a flash of white in the darkly rosy face.

Of all of us, myself and Chico included, that young girl had the clearest idea what she was doing there, the surest knowledge of where she was going. The others hoped but she knew that the difference between what she was leaving and where she was bound was worth the trouble, the expense, the risk of getting there. She might have been going to a man, or getting away from one; maybe she just had a job waiting. Whatever, she knew she had made the right decision, and her confidence – in her choice, in herself – was a much needed boost for me and probably everyone else there.

Well, maybe everyone except Chico, who was back in his own self-contained, professional little world and no more capable of appreciating this young girl's spunk than my weak but well-intentioned little joke. He acknowledged it with the faintest of smiles, and his eyes went on past me and round the walls of our travelling box before I could react to his coolness.

Well the hell for you, I thought, and leaned out. 'My name's Annie, I'm a smuggler.'

The girl's ear-to-ear beam indicated that she at least took some pleasure in my company. 'Buenas tardes, Señora.' Señora? – did she think Chico was my man, or was it merely the courtesy due to a woman of my age? 'My name is Angel, and I am no longer a hooker.'

So that was it. She'd done what was necessary to raise the money to go north, and if she wasn't exactly proud of how she was at least strong with the knowledge that she had done it herself, that she owed her future to no one. I pushed my free hand towards her. 'Angel, it's a pleasure to know you.'

The warmth and sureness in her slender grasp were the answer to a question I hadn't formulated, let alone asked. But that mutual recognition of allies was a good feeling. It was only later that it occurred to me to wonder how I would feel when we succeeded in closing this operation down, and sent Angel and the others back to the lives they had dragged themselves out of by their bootstrings.

Soon after that the rig hauled itself off the dirt road on to a proper metalled surface and gathered speed. The jolting, pitching movement ended between one breath and the next, the rattling in the chassis dropped and the hum from the wheels mounted. Only by such impressions, and the passage of time, were we able to chart our progress. After an hour darkness fell.

Until then almost the only sound in the trailer, except for occasional hurried whispers or choked, embarrassed coughing, had been that short but unapologetic exchange between Angel and myself. With the dying of the day, however, my fellow travellers came slowly out of their shells. They asked after one another's well-being and pooled adjectives to describe the journey so far. Some of them wished they had made their own way nearer to the border, to avoid the long haul in the trailer, but an authoritative voice said that was a sure way to get caught, that American agents haunted the border towns looking out for strangers from the south, and followed them to the border, and beat them and robbed them and sent them back. The smart way was to join a convoy far from the river country. The Americans couldn't follow every truck carrying cotton, or coffee, or cattle.

Chico said nothing. I wondered if he disliked himself at that moment as much as I did.

The conversation gained pace, moved on. One of the women was going to join her daughter in Abilene. This was Rosa. Her daughter had a good job managing an eating house there, and though she had no papers it was obviously all right because she'd been there for four years. Rosa was going to work in the kitchen.

Juliano was just fifteen. His father was working as a mechanic in San Diego and had sent for him. His grandmother had packed him off with enough food in his pockets to see all of us across the Rio Grande.

Felipe was a vaquero. He wanted to work with horses on a Texas ranch. He had worked with horses on a hacienda in Sonora, but his old patron died and the new patron hadn't much interest in horses, and sold most of them to pay for his swimming-pool; so Felipe found himself out of a job.

Some of them had hard-luck stories. Some of them had the promise of something better in the States. Some were just travelling hopefully. All of them gave, quite

inadvertently and without playing for sympathy, glimpses
of lives in which harshness and privation were the rule
rather than the exception. I felt ashamed in their
company: ashamed of the comfort of my home, the
security of the job I had so blithely thrown away, the
absolute certainty that once this adventure was over I
could return to a way of living that even their wildest
dreams of America did not include. If Rosa got her chance
to be an underpaid skivvy in an Abilene cafe kitchen, she
would be content and grateful. We came from different
worlds, they and I, and though I had known it
intellectually it wasn't until then that I understood what
that meant.

Most of this I was able to follow with my schoolgirl
Spanish, rusty from disuse but up to fairly basic
conversation given the occasional prompt by Angel. Chico
made no contribution, to the conversation or my
understanding. He might not have been there, except for
once when, mainly to remind myself where he was in the
dark, I asked how he was doing and he said, 'This place
stinks.'

He was absolutely right, of course, but I could have
managed without him saying it. The tiny backlight on my
watch said we'd been four hours on the road.

6

When my watch said we'd been travelling a little over five
hours the road changed suddenly again, the many wheels
bumping over some kind of a gutter and on to some kind
of a dirt track. We jounced along, familiar enough with
one another now to bounce off and cling to each other
without embarrassment, for several minutes. Then the rig
screwed round a tight double turn and hissed to a halt.
The engine shuddered and died. After five hours on the
move the stillness and the silence were almost sinister.

We waited, in the silence and the dark, quiet and still ourselves, waiting for liberation like animals or slaves. Minutes passed. We heard the cab doors slam as the crew climbed down, but it seemed an unconscionably long time before they came to bestow the same freedom on us.

Muffled, through the cotton, we could hear them talking, casually, without purpose. In my mind's eye I watched them stretch, rub at muscles weary with driving, light cigarettes, kick at the tyres. Eventually, so I supposed, they looked at one another and grimaced, and one of them said, 'Reckon we'd best let the greasers out.'

The clip grated and the hatch swung down, and a track of torchlight showed the way. The man who had loaded us raised his head momentarily through the hole. 'C'mon y'all, time to get out.'

In the faint backwash of light I sought Chico's eyes. 'Should I leave this in here?' I was holding the codex.

His glance was negligent. 'Suit yourself.' He pressed ahead of me to the hatch, leaving Angel and me to help one another make the awkward manoeuvre as best we could. For all I knew he might bear the FBI decoration for Extreme Cleverness, a gold jelly-baby rampant on a ground of silver peanuts with the motto 'I am not a crook' worked in Latin underneath, but as a minder he left a lot to be desired.

I cornered him outside and poked him in the chest with a schoolmarmy forefinger. 'You do know why you're here, do you?' I asked waspishly. 'To protect the codex – did someone mention that? Oh good, I was beginning to wonder.'

'I don't need you to tell me my job.'

'No? Well perhaps I will anyway, just for my own peace of mind. The only reason Mason agreed to let you come was that I persuaded him the codex could need more looking after than I could give it. He didn't like me bringing in someone he didn't know, that's the sort of risk he doesn't take, but he took it for the safety of the codex.

It's that important. Do you understand what I'm telling you? It's more important than anyone here.

'Don't worry about me, I can look after myself – I'll take my chances with the rest of these poor sods. But what's in this leather drum matters, and it matters enough to be worth your time and trouble thinking whether I should keep it with me or find somewhere to stash it. Jesus, we had no business bringing it. It should be in a glass case in the museum, with admiring throngs filing respectfully past. Well, that was Alvarado's decision, thank God, not mine, but I'm damned if I'm taking him back a box of bits and an explanation. That's why you're here, Chico: to guard that thing with your life.'

Resentment stiffened his body and kindled in his eyes, and he breathed softly. After a moment he spoke. 'Lady, I'll say this once so there'll be no misunderstanding. I don't give a damn about that screw of chalk and baghide. It means nothing to me. I know there are people who would lay down their lives and those of others to possess it, or protect it, or preserve it for posterity, but I'm not one of them. If it ever comes to a straight choice between that trinket and these people, it'll lose.

'Do you understand me? I'll be sorry – for your embarrassment, for Balfour's reputation, for the people trooping sadly past an empty case in the museum – but whatever its value, it's still and only an object. The people who left it also left children, and their children's children left these people. Look after your art treasure to the best of your ability, and I'll look after you; but after you, I'll be looking out for these poor sods who think they're crossing Jordan into a promised land.'

With that he swatted my finger and walked away.

We were in a yard pretty much like the first, maybe a packing-station of some kind, and there were two privies for the forty-two of us so the queues were long and, towards the end, verging on the desperate. There was also food, of a kind – tacos and cold beans, and coffee apparently brewed with old shoelaces. We had about half an hour to eat and walk round, and then they wanted to load us up again.

Chico sidled up behind me. 'Ask them for a torch.'

I sought out Blair. 'Any chance of a torch? It's as black as the duke of hell's waistcoat in there.'

He shook his head. 'Sorry. Any light would be visible between those bales at night. I don't want anybody getting the idea that this load of cotton is anything but cotton.'

He had a point. The daylight had got in, so presumably torchlight could get out.

Chico said, 'What's the smell in there?'

Blair looked at him as he had when they first met. 'Cotton. What kind of a fancy Mexican are you, you don't know what cotton smells like?'

'I know how cotton should smell, and it's not like that.'

Blair took up a deep breath. 'Well, I'm very sorry our cotton don't match up to your exacting standards, Señor – what is your name, anyway?'

There was the briefest of pauses before Chico replied. 'Colón.'

Columbus. It was so obviously an alias as to need no comment. Blair twitched a quick grin. 'Señor Colón. But we bought it more for the bulk than the quality, and the smell may be a little coarser than you're used to. Stick with it, the experience may broaden your personal horizons.' He moved away, chuckling.

We got back in the trailers.

When we were on the road again Angel said, 'It's been wet.'

'Sorry?'

'The cotton. Your friend wanted to know why it smells like this. It's been wet. it's drying out.'

I thought about it. We were getting to the end of the dry season but we weren't there yet. 'How would it get wet?'

I felt her shrug – her left shoulder was next to my right. 'How should I know? Maybe in the warehouse. They have sprinklers in case of fire. Maybe a sprinkler went off.'

'What?' It was Chico, finally honouring us with his attention. He sounded troubled. No, to be honest, he sounded downright twitchy. 'What's she saying?'

'She says,' I explained with heavy patience, 'that the cotton smells because it got sprinkled in the warehouse and it's drying out.'

'It's been wet?' He was keeping his voice low, low enough under the noise of the trailer to confine the conversation to the three of us, but clearly something was bothering him more than just the smell. 'Jesus God!'

We were back on good road. In the course of the next few hours we passed through a couple of small towns and maybe round a larger one – impressions were all we could get, from the sound and headlights of other vehicles, how close we passed to facing traffic, how many junctions we crossed where the headlamps washed down the sides of the trailer, how many times our rig had to slow down to accommodate other traffic. Midnight came and went.

Outside the temperature had been falling for nine hours and at this height and in this season the night must have been unequivocally cold, but the cotton bales were good insulation and in the narrow space between them twenty-two bodies generated enough heat to keep comfortable. It was just as well, because none of us had more than a jacket or a shawl to our backs and some of us hadn't even that.

We had first scrambled into this battery henhouse on wheels getting on for ten hours before. Most of us had been travelling all day, some of us for longer than a day. Anxiety, apprehension and discomfort notwithstanding, we were all very tired and most of us were tired enough to want to sleep. There was a groundswell of movement, growing from modest and tentative beginnings into a fairly general shuffling, bumping, begging of pardons, granting of indulgences, issuing of invitations and eventual expressions of satisfaction. People ended up lying on the seats and on the floor, or stretched their legs out to the seat opposite and leaned their heads on each other's shoulders. From a mixed bag of strangers, embarrassed by our enforced proximity, we had become as familiar as puppies in a litter.

We finally found a kind of ease, my companions and I, with Chico's legs stretched across the gap, my legs across his and Angel's head in my lap, and I was only grateful that there was no chance of a light springing up to reveal our strange abandon. I doubt if any of us actually slept, but thus we rested through the dark hours until some time after one when the rig slowed, made its familiar bouncing turn off the metalled road on to rough ground, and quickly came to a halt.

Again the long pause, the eventual grate of the latch in its keeper, the upwash of torchlight. 'We have to stay off the road a few hours. There's not enough traffic about, we'll get noticed if we go on. You can get out and stretch your legs if you want to, but there's nowhere for you to sleep except in here. There'll be something to eat about five, then we'll get back on the road.'

With the prospect of three hours before we could do anything more than relieve cramped muscles and full bladders, few of our company showed a marked anxiety to move from what comfort they had achieved. The exception was Chico, and when he dropped through the hatch and slithered out of sight I thought I'd better go too. A worrisome blurring of roles had taken place between minder and minded, but if he irritated Blair enough to get left by the roadside I would be on my own with a national treasure and my own safety to worry about. I thrust the drum into Angel's hands and followed. I was getting quite proficient at snaking in and out of this hole. I had a sudden crazy wish that 3b could see me now.

I found the two men at the front of the rig, under the frowning gaze of the big chrome grill, and already they were arguing.

Neither of them was shouting. Blair was speaking, very quietly, very seriously, and I was up with them before I could hear what he was saying.

'Son,' he was saying, 'I have told you once already and I don't expect to have to tell you again. If I get any hassle from you it's not going to matter worth a damn who sent you, I am going to break your legs and leave you in a ditch.'

'Damn you, *listen* to me,' hissed Chico, and his voice too was low. 'It isn't me you have to worry about, it's how you're going to get twenty-two people out of a hole in the bottom of a trailer travelling at fifty miles an hour when that cargo goes on fire.'

'Fire?' Horrified, I was still automatically keeping my voice to the pitch of the conversation I had joined.

Blair looked round and down in surprise. He hadn't known I was there. 'Where did you spring from?'

'From the fire-hazard back there,' I said, with what I considered commendable restraint.

'Jeez, lady,' he growled, 'the only fire-hazard round here's your greaser's head!'

'I'm telling you, Blair, you don't do something about it, that cotton's going up.'

Suddenly I understood. 'Because it's been wet?'

'Hallelujah,' said Chico, heavily.

Blair was looking from one to the other of us in a kind of baffled despair. 'It's going to catch fire because it's wet? Are you two on something?'

'Bales of cotton are like bales of hay. If they aren't dry when you stack them they can heat up inside. Spontaneous combustion: you ever hear of that?'

'Yeah. You ever hear of lippy kids getting their faces beat in?' But he was not a stupid man, he was buying time to think about it. 'Supposing you're right. What do you want me to do about it?'

'Dump the cotton. Spread it out in the sun, it'll dry OK. Pick it up again next run.'

'Yeah? And for the next three hundred miles you all sit out in the sun, waving to the peasants like a bunch of presidential candidates? Grow up, sonny.'

'Get hold of some more.'

Blair too was showing commendable restraint: he went for a short circular walk in front of the cab as an alternative to hitting him. Then he said carefully, 'It's the middle of the night. We're trying not to be noticed. Where do you suggest I find forty tons of cotton, and even if I find it how in hell am I supposed to weigh it so the axle-weights match the manifest?'

'It's the same cotton on both trailers?'

'Of course it's the same cotton!'

'Blair, I don't know what you're going to have to do, but if you don't do something you're going to incinerate these people. That cotton's heating up. I can smell it. It's night now, but tomorrow when the sun's on it the whole damn lot will go up.'

I believed him. Blair believed him too. Whatever antipathy there was between them, there was no mistaking the absolute conviction in Chico's voice, in his face. He wasn't shaking any more than he was shouting, but he was clearly afraid. If it happened he would be in there. So would I.

'OK,' said Blair, 'I'll tell you what I'll do. We'll get the bales off and reload them, with the inside ones to the outside where they can cool down. That do you?'

Chico shrugged. 'I don't know.'

'Well, sonny, you'd *better* know, because it's the best I can offer you, and it's going to be an all-night job starting now, and if I find out it wasn't necessary you'd better be somewhere else.'

The truck had pulled off the road behind a filling-station. There was no one there; it was hard to say if the place was closed down or just closed. Blair got a light rigged, and checked that it didn't show from the freeway, then got everyone off. Excepting only a couple of elderly

women and some small children, we formed up into teams
to manhandle the bales down. Blair muttered something
that I think was meant to excuse me from participating, so
I made sure of a place in the chain-gang where he could
see me sweating and slaving with the rest, and wonder just
how close to his boss I was.

Angel was in there too, her sleeves rolled up to the
elbows, so we left the priceless national treasure with an
old lady who had probably spent ten years saving for this
trip and would undoubtedly drop it in the road if she had
to waddle after an errant toddler.

It took us over an hour to strip the load, turn the bales
then heave them laboriously back into place. Blair directed
the reconstruction, with Chico on top acting as head
gaffer. My shoulders turned slowly to a slab of fire. My
hands were chafed by the bindings which offered the only
grip. The crew, who to their credit didn't stand back and
watch, had heavy chrome-leather gloves. Fibres from the
cotton filled the air we breathed and filled our lungs. The
work got harder as coughing, blisters and sheer exhaustion
began to take their toll of our numbers. After a ten-minute
break we started on the second trailer.

The last half-hour I worked in a daze, taking hold of
whatever was offered to me and passing it on to anyone
who looked they might like it. Sometimes I couldn't
remember whether the bales were supposed to be coming
down or going up. Getting them aloft was far harder,
fighting gravity instead of using it. When the stack reached
head height it was impossible, in the absence of an elevator,
to get the bales up by hand. We attached ropes for the men
on top to haul them up by. It was back-breaking work. Like
Blair, I hoped Chico had been right about the danger.
Even so I ended up hating him with every throb of my
lacerated palms and aching back, with every spasm of my
polluted lungs.

At last, standing there waiting for a bale which never
came, I realised we had finished. I looked round, vacantly.

The ground which had been covered with cotton was now covered only with other weary, vacant people. The old ladies who had watched had turned to preparing an early breakfast. The codex sat alone on an upturned oil-drum while a five-year-old pondered its potential as a football. I rescued it.

I saw Blair watching me. Too tired to do anything else, I nodded him a brief grin. He smiled back. The poor man looked impressed.

Chico appeared, literally swaying on his feet with weariness, and flopped beside me on a plank bench I had found. His eyes were bothering him, full of the same cotton dust which clogged our noses and throats. He rubbed at them incessantly until I got water off one of the old women and soaked a handkerchief. I went to wash his eyes out, as I had done so often for the thuglets of 3b after fights in the sandpit, but he jerked away from me as if I had tried to hurt him, and took the cloth and turned his back on me, hunching over the wet rag pressed to his face.

I knew he was tired, I knew he was sore; I was tired too, not least of his moods which were not so much mercurial as manic. 'Chico, what the hell's the matter with you?'

He half turned, darting me a hunted animal look that only by the merest chance was caught by the light as one of Blair's crew brought down the spotlamp. His eyes were red from rubbing, but the startling thing was that their irises were no longer brown. They were a pale, almost luminous hazel in the artificial light. They were, to within a shade or two, the same colour as mine.

So it all fell into place. The way he never looked at me. The strange ambivalence of his attitude. Even the absurd alias. Joshua Cade's inability to cope with my questions. The despair of the hospital, which was not how much it hurt but how little. And other things which hadn't made sense at the time and now did. I made an effort to breathe quietly, watching him wonder, then fear, then accept the fact that I knew.

He said, inconsequentially, 'Contact lenses. The dust gets underneath – '

I said, 'You unutterable bastard. Why didn't you *tell* me?'

Chris

1

My brother Cristóbal continued rinsing out his eyes: partly perhaps because they still hurt, partly so that the handkerchief would muffle his words, but mostly so that he didn't have to look at me. There was no one beside us, no one paying us any attention, and enough quiet hubbub around the truck to prevent our voices carrying. We were able to speak freely for the first time in sixteen hours. We were interrupted only once, when one of the old women came over with food for us and smiled toothlessly before leaving us alone again.

Chico said, 'How much do you know?'

I could barely keep the break out of my voice, barely contain the anger. 'What you told me – you and Joshua Cade. Until this moment I believed you were dead.'

So he began at the beginning. 'The first time I did this trip – not with Mason's mules – it was for real. I was one sixteen-year-old wetback among God knows how many that year, and I got as far as Fort Worth before the reality of the American Dream began to dawn on me. I saw a lot of misery in those six months, not only among illegals like myself. There was money – hell, there was money, you only had to look in the parking-lots and shop windows, but it wasn't for me or the likes of me. I damn near starved; I did end up in hospital.'

But not from starvation, I thought, or only in a way. But he must have forgotten that I knew about that because he passed over it with no further reference.

'That was where I met Flores. He was doing what I do now. He knew I was undocumented, of course. He wanted to know how I'd come north – who helped, what way I came, how much it cost, where they picked me up, where they left me.'

His voice had sunk very low, not only because of the absolute need not to be overheard. He was talking out of some kind of reverie, and even I – close as I was and intent upon his words – had trouble following them.

'You don't do that,' he said. 'You don't ever do that. It's the first thing the coyotes impress on you – you don't ever give them away. Most people travel with them again and again: if they find out you talked about them they make an example of you. So you don't. The Americans send you back – they call it their Revolving Door policy – and the guards on the Mexican side rob you of most anything you got left, but still you don't talk. You start getting the money together for another try. Twelve hours in the tobacco fields earns you four dollars, if there is any work. For four or five months there is no work.

'So I told him. I was sixteen years old; I was hurt, I was sick and I was scared. He said they'd throw me out of the hospital if I didn't help him. I didn't know my father' – after a quick, furtive glance at me he changed that – 'your father would pay for me. I thought I was going to die.

'That's all it was at first. I was talking to save my skin. I don't know when Flores got the idea of recruiting me, but over the next couple of weeks he started talking about my future. What I was going to do when I got better. How there was nothing for me in Mexico, even if the coyotes didn't get me. How he could fix me up with some education and a career if I worked for him. And he was right, I had nowhere else to go.

'When I got out of the hospital he sent me to Boston, to school. I think I was the only Spanish-speaker in Boston. I guess he wanted to keep me away from the border. It was a good choice: I learned good English there, and their idea of a vicious threat was black-balling you at the country club. I did OK in school. I wanted to be an engineer. Flores had other ideas, of course, but I think I'd have fought him off long enough to go to college except that the coyotes got him alone in Tijuana one night and broke his back. He lived for eight months. That was how long it took him to get enough strength to cut his wrists.

'I never much cared for him when he was alive – he was a ruthless, exploitive man – but I found I wanted the bastards who killed him more than I wanted to build pretty bridges. I teamed up with his successor and we did some good work. We never got the ones who killed Flores, but we got plenty more. I travelled with them, he arranged the welcoming committee. Now I work with Joshua Cade, but the job's pretty much the same.'

Incredibly, he stopped there. I don't know if he thought he had told me everything that mattered – which is possible, because explaining and justifying the work he did had accounted for a substantial part of our few conversations, clearly it was something that concerned him – or if it was difficult for him to go on. But however difficult, however painful, he wasn't leaving it at that.

'Chico, I was told you were dead. *You* told me my brother was dead. *Why?*'

He looked at me, our green eyes meeting, and there were depths of guilt and regret where before I had seen only shadows. It took him a moment to say it. 'I didn't think you'd care. I didn't expect the news to reach anyone who would care. They thought they'd killed me – Mason or whoever. It was necessary, for my safety, for the success of the job, that they go on believing that. I switched IDs with one of the men in the truck.'

'Tell me what happened.'

His eyes veered away again and his voice sank back to that dream-state pitch, like a tired poet telling a last sad saga across the embers of a dying fire. 'I got careless, or maybe unlucky, I don't know which. They figured out they had a spy aboard.

'They had a description, but it couldn't have been much cop because there were seven of us it fitted. The eldest was about forty, the youngest seventeen; one of them had only one eye. They separated us from the rest of the train and took us into a shed. We heard the truck we'd come in drive away.

'They spent three hours trying to work out which of us it was. They said they'd kill us all if I didn't give myself up. I thought they were bluffing. They left us alone for a time, so the real wetbacks could find the phony one. But we were all strangers, from different parts of the country, and my background was as real as anyone's.

'There was a kid called Cachuchas, they started to think it could be him. They said he had to own up to the coyotes to save the rest of us. He swore on his mother's grave it wasn't him, and when the coyotes came back nobody said anything. They had a go at beating it out of us, but I've been done over by experts and nobody else knew anything so they were none the wiser.

'Finally they said they must have been mistaken. They apologised for the delay and loaded us aboard another truck. We crossed the border and we thought we were safe, and when they kept on driving we thought they were just taking us somewhere quiet to let us out. They drove up into the hills and got off the road and stopped. We waited for them to come and open the door. After a couple of minutes the front end of the trailer kind of shuddered and the couplings parted, and the cab drove away without us.'

For a long time no one had spoken. Then they had taken refuge in bravado: the coyotes were trying to scare them into revealing the spy, they'd come back in half an hour and demand to know who it was. When there was still no answer they'd be set free.

'I thought so too. I still thought they were bluffing. God help me, I thought it was a bluff.'

Time passed. The steel box lost all its heat to the desert

night. The sides burned the unprotected skin. They tried to force the door, without success. They couldn't even force the grille at the top of the door. There was no light, no heat, no fresh air. After two hours they began to face the possibility that the coyotes – he called them that when he was speaking from the standpoint of the illegals; speaking as a US government agent he called them mules – would not return, and that they would die there.

They were afraid; and then they were also angry. Their anger was not directed at the man who had abandoned them, only in the rather vague and impersonal way in which you might be angry that it rained on your parade; mostly they blamed the spy who had brought the situation about by refusing to sacrifice himself. They blamed the young man Cachuchas.

'They started laying into him – seriously, almost in silence, with their fists and their boots and the buckle-ends of their belts. He was screaming at them to stop, crying with the pain. It didn't matter any more, we were all going to die, so I told them it was me. For a minute they didn't know what to do about that. They kept on looking at the boy as if they'd sooner have gone on beating him. Then the roof of the truck fell on me.'

That was the last clear memory he had. The rest was pieced together from what Joshua Cade found when his people discovered the trailer and forced the locked doors.

Frightened and frustrated, the doomed men had beaten Chico unconscious and finally slung his body into a corner of the trailer. The skin of his cheek froze to the metal where his face lay against the side wall. Then they had set about relieving their distress as best they could. Driven by instinct as much as by the biting cold and impervious dark, they got together what scraps they could find, in the trailer and about their own persons, and they lit a fire. It killed them as surely as, if more slowly than, a bullet to the brain.

When Cade opened the truck he found six lifeless bodies, slumped in easy postures around the ashes of the fire as if they had simply gone to sleep, lulled by the warmth and the smoke and not realising, or perhaps not caring, that they had created a monster which was devouring their air. And then in the corner, comatose, rigid with cold, cyanotic but still somehow alive, he found Chico.

'They reckoned it was the cold that saved me.' In his scarred face and in the low notes of his quiet voice were still the wonder and the horror of surviving where so many had died. It seemed incredible to me that these events had taken place within the last few weeks. I had wondered at his moods: now I wondered that he wasn't still being drip-fed tranquillisers in a psychiatric ward. 'Apparently your body slows down at low temperatures – you bleed less, you breathe less. There must have been enough air left, in the corner away from the fire, to keep one cold body ticking over when six warm bodies had already exhausted their needs and died. Even the fire hadn't enough oxygen to keep burning.'

And it was in the back of the truck, before they had moved either the six dead bodies or the one live one, while the paramedics were still working on the survivor with oxygen masks and stimulants and swaddling him in astronauts' foil blankets, that the great deceit was born. And Joshua Cade was the author of it.

'Obviously the mules had caught up with me,' said Chico, his voice soft to talk of his own death. 'Obviously they reckoned they'd dealt with me. All it needed was official confirmation and they'd strike a line through my name and description, I'd be as safe among them as anyone in my trade ever is. He was thinking of me. He didn't even know about you. We none of us carried papers, and there was no one to contradict him, so he identified Cachuchas as Cristóbal Baez, US government agent, and that was the story that went out. Then he sat by my bed for eight hours until I came round, in case I said anything that would make a nonsense of it.'

He was worried, when Cade explained, that Señora Delgado might be told, but there seemed scant likelihood. She had heard nothing about his work while he was alive. He never imagined that word of his death would reach his father's family across the Atlantic. That was Cade's fault too. He slipped an old letter he had taken from Chico's rooms into Cachuchas's clothing, where a mortuary attendant subsequently discovered it and made rude remarks about the inability of Border Patrol to find anything that wasn't actually singing 'South of the Border'. He had not expected that a clerk in administration would take it on himself to write to the return address.

'It wasn't my idea – I was in no shape to have ideas about then – but it was me Cade did it for, and anyway I could have ended it before it went much further. I didn't want to. It gave us an edge, an advantage we could use. You don't get so many you can afford to turn your nose up at one. We went with it. The kid in the morgue was Cristóbal Baez and I was free to be anyone I needed to be. But you sure as hell knocked Cade on his butt when you marched into his office.'

I could imagine. As far as Cade knew Cristóbal had no relations: when he heard that a pushy female one had turned up on the far side of the Atlantic and was on her way to confront him he must have wondered who up there had it in for him. He must have –

'He must have talked to you.'

The green gaze was steady. 'Oh yes. That was one decision that was mine. It didn't come easy. I thought it was best. I didn't expect – well, you. I couldn't imagine you grieving over me. We'd never met, we meant nothing to each other. Whatever shock the news of my death had been was already in the past. It would have been no kindness then to tell you who I was. I knew whoever was responsible for the killings would be looking to confirm my death, would know you had arrived. There was always the danger he'd use you to check it out. And that's what happened, I don't think that invitation to Sugar Valley was anything to do with entertaining strangers. If you'd known I was alive – '

'You think I'd have told him?' My voice stayed almost calm but outrage surged within me.

'No. But I think you could have been hurt refusing to, and I think anyway he'd have known. There was another reason. I knew I was coming back here. This is a high-risk profession: I don't plan on dying but it could happen. It seemed to me that if you had to lose a bastard half-brother once was enough, and better if you'd never met him.'

He looked up then with a strange, almost wistful little smile. 'Though I couldn't resist the chance of meeting you. I thought I was safe enough – the only thing Cade had let slip was that we have the same eyes, and I could always look the other way. I thought I could just talk to you for a few minutes, then send you home and nobody any the wiser only me. But you aren't that easy to get rid of, are you?'

'So I've been told.'

'And to be honest, I'm not sure how hard I tried.'

'You said you didn't like me very much.'

He grinned back – tired, still tired, but with a kind of relief or release in him, as if he'd been able to shed one burden at least. 'I lied.'

Finally he surrendered the handkerchief and let me look at his eyes and bandage his torn hands. I whispered, 'What do I call you?'

His eyes flared briefly in the remaining light. 'For as long as this goes on, Chico Colón is the only name of mine you know. But if I'm still alive at the end of the month, my pay cheque will be made out to Chris Baez.'

2

We returned to the trailers at about six and pulled out shortly afterwards. There still wasn't much on the road, but enough probably for our rig to pass unremarked.

It was noticeably colder inside the trailer now. The comfortable fug built up by our bodies, and perhaps the less desirable heat given off by the damp cotton, had been dispersed and if it was spring the nights were still bitterly cold. We huddled together for warmth long after the sun had begun its progress up the sky.

But except in the most superficial, bodily sense I cared nothing for the cold, or the confinement, or even the safety of the codex which had occupied me almost exclusively until then. My mind was in turmoil; not on the surface, where an almost unnatural calm prevailed, but in the worm-heart of that silken cocoon. In the innermost place where I lived, where I hung up my conceits and defences and watched myself on the TV in my dressing-gown, the blinds had been thrown up, the cushions scattered, and the cat was screaming round the walls. My mind was a raucous chaos, a Bosch madhouse of whirling images and fragmentary cries, directionless, dimensionless. My mind was twisting in a kaleidoscope, lacerated by the lancet edges of the spinning shards.

Through it all two giant facts cast sprawling shadows: that my brother, whose murder I had come six thousand miles to grieve and avenge, was no more dead than I was; and that my righteous anger had projected us into the thick of enemies who, if they came once to suspect what I now knew, would not hesitate to kill us both. With an American agent in tow and the determination to bring down the man who owned the truck we were travelling in, I had of course known I was in some hazard. I had supposed that if I kept my head and played my part, no one would guess that my involvement was more or other than the obvious.

But in the company of a man already supposedly dead at the hands of these same people? – a man, moreover, whose relationship to me made it impossible for me to claim ignorance and be believed. It happened to be true that, until an hour ago, I had known Chico Colón for my brother's colleague and never guessed he was my brother. But if my life came to depend on someone believing that, I was already lost. They'd still be giggling when they buried us.

Even while I was thinking thus, I felt myself consumed by a dreadful shame. The fairy had waved her wand and the wish had been granted: the dead man was alive again, and not only alive but here where I could touch him and know him. And all I could think of was how much more dangerous it was having a live brother than a dead one!

Then there was the quetion of whether I liked him. It hadn't mattered when I thought he was dead: I had cared whether he was content, fulfilled, happy, but not whether he was nice. Now I found myself worrying about it. Apart from occasional brief flashes of kindness, he had treated me during our short acquaintance with lack of interest, disdain, detachment and some harshness. He had been short to the point of brusqueness only excepting those occasions on which he had been downright rude. Though I had not known him, he had known me; yet he had offered no friendship, no warmth, and only such protection as had been expedient in the light of our task. He had behaved like a – like a –

Let's face it, he had behaved pretty much like a brother. It didn't matter whether I liked him or not, whether he liked me. You can choose your friends and your lovers, but family come unpicked and unbidden. You can love them or loathe them, try to ignore them, reject and disown them. You can stop sending them Christmas cards and strike them out of your will. What you can't do is strike them out of your genes. They're in there for good – also for bad and indifferent. They're a part of you. My brother Cristóbal – Chico, Chris, whatever he happened to be calling himself – was part of me, and had been since the moment I learned of his existence. It didn't matter what I thought of him, or he of me. We were bound, both of us, by our father's memory and chromosomes. We were family. There was nothing more to say.

When the sun was up it was lighter in the trailer than the previous day. Deliberately or inadvertently, probably the former, Chris had left more gaps as he was rebuilding the load. I thought it was our comfort he had in mind. Then I realised, watching the obsessive way he moved round these fractional slits, poised at back-breaking angles to watch the monstrous brown and grey roadscape roll past, that he was trying to plot our course and the extra light and air, while pleasant, were incidental.

Also from watching him, our fellow travellers saw there was an in-flight entertainment on offer, and most of them over the next hour picked their careful way through the sprawled bodies to have a look out. I don't think anybody did it twice: there was as near nothing to see as made no difference. The best view I achieved was of the tarmac road pouring behind us, the tail of the following trailer as we swept round a bend, blue distant mountains crouching on our spoor, and dingy fields growing something that already looked dead and stretched uninterrupted for miles. I couldn't imagine what Chris could see that would enable him to pinpoint where we were. But I was anxious in case any of our company should wonder at his persistence and mention it to the men up front.

I suppose that was naive of me. Chris knew these people as I did not: gut deep, soul deep. He had worked with them and travelled with them, these people or their near relations. He had lived with them, grown up with them; in simple fact, he was one of them. They had more in common, though they were illegals and he was a government agent, than any of them had with the North Americans in the cab. The very word they used to describe those men, whom they were paying for a valuable service, defined the relationship and the situation. They called them coyotes. No one in that trailer was about to mention Chris's odd behaviour to the coyotes. We were safe with them.

We stopped again mid-morning – briefly, there wasn't time to both eat and queue for the loo, so all those agile (or desperate) enough to head up the queue knocked up roughshod sandwiches from the scraps on offer and ate on their feet during the long wait. We amused ourselves trying to identify what we were eating. Angel was reduced to hysterics by something she swore was a pickled cicada and I munched my way stoically through what looked, and for all I know also tasted, like a hyacinth bulb. I thought, This is one of those occasions I shall look back on in years to come; and that little sod of a realist who lives inside me and hoots derisively at my least inclination to romance added maliciously: With loathing, revulsion and a marked tendency to throw up.

We were returning to the trailers when some sort of an altercation broke out near the rear. We all looked round. Blair made directly for the spot with long raking strides, and Chris indirectly by means of a determined hip-swerving sidle. With my burden tucked underneath my arm, a little like a White Lady's head, I followed.

One of the illegals in the second trailer was pinned with his back to the wheel by the presence of Blair's men, the three of them surrounded by a dense ring of interested people, half curious and half afraid. Before Blair they parted; Chris wriggled through in his wake, and I stayed on the periphery, on tiptoe, grateful that the Mexican is not one of the world's taller people. On tiptoe behind Watusi I should have learnt nothing. As it was I could see and hear enough to follow what was happening.

The man was carrying drugs. Cocaine. He had come from the south with enough cocaine in the lining of his clothes to become the major industry in any number of small American towns. He was trying to tell them it was to feed a personal habit, but a personal habit on that scale would have killed an elephant. Blair took the flat white packets from him, slapping his hands away when he tried to resist and thumping him a couple of times as an afterthought.

'From here on out,' he growled, 'you ride up front with us, and if anybody asks you're a hitcher we picked up in Saltillo.' He stalked back to the cab, hustling the man in front of him, and the rest of us returned to the trailers.

When we were under way again I asked Chris, 'What did you make of that?'

'How do you mean?'

'Blair. I didn't have him marked for a man who'd object to drugs on principle.'

He didn't exactly laugh in my face, but his expression was eloquent and not flattering. 'Principle?'

I backed off, but not all the way. 'All right, maybe principle's not the word; but principle or pragmatism, the fact remains – '

'The fact undoubtedly remains,' said Chris, quietly sardonic, his tone and his green eyes mocking me, 'that somewhere on this rig Blair's carrying enough cocaine, and heroin, and probably cannabis too although the profits on that aren't what they were, to send two colleges, a med school and a military academy into orbit. That gives him three very good reasons for not wanting his passengers to carry as well. Availability governs the street value. Also, he doesn't want to be boarded because of José Rivera's indiscretions. When Josh Cade's people search a vehicle, they take it down to the axle bearings.'

'José Rivera?'

'The Colombian. I know him, he's done this before.'

'Jesus Christ! Does he know you?'

He grinned, without much mirth. 'He didn't last time we met. He just may have guessed since.'

'And now he's travelling up front and badly in need of something to trade.'

'Yeah. Interesting, isn't it?' He went on with his analysis. 'Finally, he doesn't want to spend infinite time and caution distributing what he brings in, only to have Rivera picked up for peddling it on street corners like shoelaces and offering information on how he got there for a reduced sentence. No, I don't somehow think José Rivera will be crossing any more rivers.'

'They'll kill him?' There was something obscurely reassuring about the way my voice ran up on the horror of it, as if I had not spent the last week dealing – emotionally, intellectually and practically – with the consequences of violent death.

Chris shrugged, slightly with his shoulders, more with his eyebrows. 'Maybe. Maybe they'll just do him over and dump him. It's a damn nuisance.'

Nuisance? Yes, well, I dare say some sociologist somewhere has written lengthily on the nuisance value of murder. 'Why?'

His eyes warned me we shouldn't be talking about it. 'If they leave him alive they'll have to change the route, set up new pick-ups and stops he won't know about. As long as he lives there's the danger – more than that, the likelihood – that some time he'll offer to sell them to get himelf out of trouble.'

'You're saying they *should* kill him!'

Again that ambivalent facial shrug. 'From a purely professional point of view they should. They can change the route – it'll cost money but it can be done – but he'll have seen a lot of faces in the last twenty-four hours. It's a small world on the border. Some day he'll see one of them again, and next time he's facing twelve years for a narcotics bust he'll want to trade.'

'But we've all seen those faces.'

'It's different. The drugs make it different. These people get picked up as illegals, they won't even be prosecuted. It costs too much. They'll be shipped to the nearest bit of border and chucked out. They'll be interviewed but they won't say anything. Why would they? They've nothing to gain and everything to lose. They can always try again, once they've got the money together, as long as the carrier is still in business. If he's been closed down or had to move on, they'll find it harder, and more expensive, and more likely to go wrong: they risk being robbed as well as ripped off. Better the devil you know. As long as all they face is deportation, they have a vested interest in protecting their carrier.'

But not Rivera. And of course, not us. The Colombian's life hung by a thread because of the risk that one day he might be backed into a corner where he would betray them. Chris and I were here specifically for that purpose. He really hadn't been joking when he wondered if he'd live long enough to collect his pay. I felt the blood drain into my shoes. These same people had abandoned seven men to their deaths because they suspected one of them was a spy. They didn't take chances. The Colombian was as good as dead, and it wouldn't take much of a slip on our part for my brother and me to join him.

Forty minutes into the journey the rig slowed and turned right, and the road surface changed from tarmac to dirt, and a couple of minutes after that we heard the cab door open and quickly close. Chris shot to his feet and hurdled his way down to the rear, pressing his eye to one of the apertures he had left. Everyone in the trailer watched him in silence. They knew what was happening. They were waiting only for confirmation.

After a moment he stood back and said in Spanish, 'Señor Rivera isn't coming any further.' He made his way back up the trailer, more carefully, without the spring, apologising for his reckless progress of the moment before. No one complained. No one spoke.

When he sat down again, heavily, his face wooden, I murmured, 'Was he dead?'

He raised his eyes momentarily to meet mine. 'Unless he keeps his brain in his backside.'

The sun had climbed up the right-hand side of the trailer

and settled on the roof. The temperature inside had climbed too, partly from the sun, partly with the confined heat of twenty-two bodies packed in cottonwool. Outside it was cooler. Though the road had been downhill from Mexico City we were still among mountains, cruising gently down the spine of the Americas.

As the temperature rose, so did the concentration of carbon dioxide in the air. Without the extra ventilation provided by Chris's secret apertures, it would have been intolerable. As it was, every breath had first been drawn by five other people and my body marked its disapproval with a dull, nagging headache. From the furrowed brows and wafted hankies around me, I supposed everyone else was feeling much the same.

Except for the novelty. Some of the people in that trailer had made this journey a couple of times a year, maybe for years. Even as they travelled north they knew there was a good chance they'd be picked up and sent back – not so much on the road, where the expertise of people like Blair who knew how to avoid that was what they were paying for, but later, in the hotels and restaurants where they would work and the hispanic ghettos where they would live. Immigration knew where to look for them, knew where they were vulnerable. They might buy a fake card for fifty dollars only to discover they also needed a fake driving licence because Highway Patrol would check that, in the process generally referred to as 'looking for browns'. They could be careful, they could be lucky, but every year a whole lot of them would be found and sent back. They didn't take it personally. It was a fact of life; and so was this dreary, uncomfortable, expensive, occasionally dangerous journey. If they wanted American wages it was part of the price they had to pay – and pay, and pay again if need be.

And Chris? He didn't do this two or three times a year, depending on how sharp Immigration were. He had done it, by his own admission, maybe fifty times. At least once he had almost died doing it – and in circumstances not dissimilar to this, locked in an airless box. I found myself watching him covertly, wondering what was going through his mind. He was no more immune to fear than I was, and I didn't believe he was inured to it either. He worked through it, despite it; possibly he worked the better for it. But that didn't answer what was, to me, the central point: *how* do you cope, on a regular basis, with that kind of fear? How do fighter pilots keep flying into battle? How do infantrymen keep going over the top? How do spies spy?

Skydivers can jump out of aeroplanes because of their belief in their own skill and that of all the other experts committed to getting them safely to the ground. Racing drivers go faster and faster because they believe that accidents aren't fortuitous, they're the result of somebody's mistake, and essentially their safety lies in their own hands. And then you get the rank amateur who goes into something in a fit of anger or bravado, without appreciating what's involved, and afterwards has no choice but to see it through as best she may.

But what about the people who do appreciate the risks; who know that, apart from their own small fund, all the skill and the expertise and the talent is ranged against them, concerted to thwart their purpose and achieve their destruction; who know what is involved, and have the choice, and still go in to bat? What about the fighter pilots, the infantrymen, the spies and my brother Chris? How the hell do you cope with that kind of fear, without being consumed by it?

Closely as I watched him – covertly, still covertly, the last thing I needed was for him to look up and ask what I was staring at – I could find no answer in my brother's face. He looked as all of them looked: tired, uncomfortable, apprehensive. Unremarkable. Under the stain his face was still bruised from the beating he had taken at Sugar Valley. Under the bruises the scars he had incurred freezing his life away in the Sarajevo hills were still healing. And under the scars – what was happening there, deep within him, in his heart and his brain and his belly? What had brought him here?

Angel said, plaintively, because she too had a headache and this was the last straw, 'Something's burning.'

I looked at her, wondering what she meant. Immediately, as if at a signal, a glowing ember fell between the planks holding our roof up and landed in my lap.

3

I had yelped, shot to my feet, brushed it down and stamped on it before the realisation sank in that this was not one of 3b's little witticisms, like the spring-loaded frog or the electric stool, but was for real. We were on fire. Chris had been right: the cotton had been ready to go up. Turning it had delayed the crisis, but under the full gaze of the midday sun the conditions for spontaneous combustion had been met. Or perhaps a spark from the exhaust stack, or a cigarette end tossed from a south-bound vehicle, had provided the stimulus. It hardly mattered now. The roof over our heads was on fire and we were travelling at fifty miles an hour sealed inside a potential inferno which the men in the cab gave no indication of having noticed.

Chris said quietly, 'We have to get out of here.'

More than anything else, even the tinder smouldering in my lap, that sparse statement of basic principle brought home to me the extremity of our situation. He said it in Spanish.

But Spanish or English, it was one thing to say and quite another to do. The only way out was the way in, the hatch in the floor, between the thundering wheels, over the pouring road. That the bolt was on the outside was immaterial: even could we have forced it, our only reward would have been a quicker death smeared along a Mexican freeway than the slow incineration in store for us here above. If the rig stopped, of course, we could all be out inside a minute. But as long as it kept rolling there was no way we could escape alive.

With a dignity that, looking back, fills me with admiration I fixed Chris with a stern sisterly eye and said, 'If you have any ideas about this, now would be a good time to air them.'

There was nothing you could call panic in the trailer. Everyone was by now aware of the situation, fully aware of the implications of that little stamped-out sputtering wick, but there was no screaming, no hysterics, only a long profound silence finally broken by a woman softly crying in despair and a man praying, just audibly and with deadly serious intent.

As I had known he would – as, with less reason, everyone in the trailer had somehow known he would – my brother took command. I don't know what language he was thinking in now; mostly he was communicating in English, low quick terse English that wasted no time on regional decoration. Even in the dread of those moments I could spare an inward grin for a half-Welsh, half-Mexican cowboy talking rapid Boston English. Also, I was proud of him.

'We can't go through the floor. We can't go through the sides – the ribs will keep the bales from moving. The top's on fire, we know that. Our best chance is punching a hole in the back. If we can push even one bale out, I can get through.'

'And do what?' If he did get through he'd be left clinging to the cargo ropes, any or all of which might be in the process of burning through where they ran out of sight over the topmost bales. If the ropes gave he would fall under the following trailer. Even if they held, he would have to claw his way round the corner and up the side of the trailer to raise the alarm. It was certainly possible, provided we could shift a bale. It was also bloody dangerous. So, of course, was doing nothing. 'Maybe Blair will notice in a minute?'

'In a minute the whole damn lot could go up. I don't think they'll be able to see or smell anything until it's too late to matter. The fire's on top and the slipstream's fanning it backwards. The first Blair will know is when another rig signals him he has a trailer ablaze. We can't wait for that.'

Again, he was right. However the fire had started, it wasn't going to end with a bit of charred cotton stamped to the floor. We had to get out, quickly, whatever the risk; only I so much wished there was someone else to run that risk. Not five minutes before I had been philosophising deeply on the nature of fear. Now I was plumbing its depths in person. I had been afraid of being caught but that, together with a marked dislike of spiders, had diminished to a perspective point, an abstraction, compared with the pressing new reality.

There is probably no fear as immediate or urgent or universally instinctive as the fear of being burned. But even that was not sufficient to eclipse totally the fear that I also had of losing my brother again. I had grieved for him when I did not know him, discovered him where I had not expected him: there seemed to be a pattern there which led with cruel inevitability to finding him only in order to lose him again. I am not a superstitious woman, touch wood, even though my Celtic background makes it uphill work at times, and I struggled to put the thought out of my mind.

But I would have given anything to have another of those tough young men stand up and say that, since by a lucky chance he was a trained circus artist, used to performing such feats from childhood, it was obvious that he and not Chris must be the one to go. Of course, none of them did. We were clear out of circus artists that trip. Nobody said anything. I rather resented them for that. There were young men there as well equipped as Chris for the physical exertion required, and just then stronger and fitter too. But it wasn't their job, and somehow – without knowing why – they all recognised that it was his.

Hands, shoulders and feet failed to shift any of the four or six bales that would have served, so they carved one apart with knives. We covered our faces with masks improvised from scarves and handkerchiefs to keep the dancing fibres out of our lungs. One on each side – there was no room for more – Chris and Felipe hacked into the chosen bale until their arms disappeared up to the shoulder and the cotton from the hole, released from the pressure of baling, puffed up round our feet like the entrails of a butchered duvet. The heat in the narrow gallery rose as the oxygen level fell. The two men streamed sweat as they worked, silently, with an urgent application that was grim rather than desperate. The planks over our heads grew warm to the touch, and the scent of burning seeped through the cracks with increasing if subtle insistency. The truck rolled on regardless.

Suddenly they were through. Chris, leaning his weight on his knife, suddenly met no resistance and shot head-first into the hole with a grunt of surprise. Felipe, grinning in triumph, grabbed his shirt and pulled him back. Not that there was any danger of him going straight through: it took them minutes after that to widen the hole sufficiently to take his shoulders. It would have taken forever to get John Wayne out. But the air improved rapidly once the vent was cut, even if I had the nasty suspicion that the extra oxygen was also fuelling the fire.

Then he was gone, head first and face up, groping above him for the baling cords that would be his only handhold until he turned the corner. His legs stuck back through the bale until he was confident of his grip. His boots needed soling. Then he drew his knees up to his chest and hauled himself out, and we heard the hiss in his teeth as his weight fell on his chafed hands. As he moved sideways towards the corner there was a brief access of light into the trailer before Felipe dived into the tunnel in his wake, worming through until the top of his body was in the open where he could watch and maybe offer an urgently needed hand.

I went to the side and stood on tiptoe at one of Chris's spyholes. I could see nothing, but when he got this far his body would cut off the light and I would know he was still safe. If he got this far. If he fell, and fell away from the wheels, and the rig was running hard by the side of the road, there was a rough bank running down to a ditch that might break his fall. Or it might break his back.

Felipe called out, 'He's made the corner.' There was a thick burr of tension in the vaquero's voice. I still couldn't see anything. But the steady meter of our progress was broken then by creaks and groans in the chassis as the rig braked, sending each of us swaying or lurching forward, and when I regained my watching post I could see the barren landscape wheeling before me.

I screamed, 'He's turning off!'

I don't think anyone in the trailer appreciated the significance of this, or the reason for the horror in my voice. To be fair, I'm not sure why I recognised the danger so quickly — I had no previous experience of articulated lorries. But it flashed up in my mind's eye like one of those TV safety shorts they put on before the midday news, when real advertisers know that anybody at home is just serving lunch. As clearly as that I saw that when an artic turns the coupling provides the constant, with the two units separating at their outside corners and converging at their inner ones.

I didn't know how sharp a turn we were making, or how closely those inside corners would approach, but I did know my brother was spreadeagled across one of them and clinging on for dear life.

Felipe, who could see with his eyes what I had seen in my mind, saw the danger too and shouted a warning. I shouted too, as if my voice could carry through the bales to a man hurtling sideways through a fifty-miles-per-hour slipstream. I felt Angel grip my hand and put her arm round my shoulders, responding to my distress though unsure of its cause, and bit off the cry. We braced ourselves against the turning pressure of the bales.

It could have been only seconds, and not many of those,

but God! those seconds stretched until they sang. I waited for his scream, for the snap of his bones. Then Felipe wormed back inside, his face drawn with shock, grey with relief. 'It's all right. He got past the corner.'

From then on I had almost no knowledge of his progress. Except for the few seconds when his body, spread and sidling like a crab's, blocked out my light I could not tell where he was, or even if he was still with us. He could have fallen and unless he timed it perfectly neither me at my peep-hole nor Felipe hanging awkwardly between our trailer and the next would have seen. We waited for some sign that he had reached the cab but none came. The road was getting rougher but the rig was not slowing. If anything it was gaining speed.

So was the fire above our heads. Felipe could see showers of sparks and clumps of charred material flying off the top. Some of them hit the front and top of the following trailer. There seemed every likelihood that we should soon have two fires for the price of one. Twice more we got sudden falls of embers on our heads. The second time Rosa's scarf, that lay around her shoulders and she held to her face to filter the growing smell of smoke from her nostrils and some of the mounting fear in her face from our eyes, caught fire and Angel snatched it from her and stamped it to the floor under the platform soles of her high-heeled boots.

Then, when I had all but despaired of Chris reaching his goal, the rig put in another sharp turn and immediately braked hard, lurching to a halt amid noisy scattering stones. Moments later the hatch in the floor was swinging free. Half of us went out that way, half through the hole carved through the bales at the back.

The people from the second trailer were disembarking too, not quite as quickly as us because they didn't know what we knew. They hastened noticeably when they saw the flames mounting from the top of our load and starting on top of theirs.

And indeed it was a spectacular sight. The flames must have been very hot, because they were almost invisible in the bright sunshine, just shimmering columns of blue and gold incandescence dancing vertically now the rushing air of the slipstream no longer pressed them back along the roofline. The smoke too was climbing now, black and high, a signal that would soon be visible for miles if it was not already. Everyone stood watching. No effort was made to douse the fire: it was too obvious that none would succeed. We had escaped with our lives. For the moment no one cared about burnt belongings or the ashes of dreams.

All I cared about for that moment was Chris. My eyes skimmed over the gathering, seeking him. I couldn't find him. I saw Blair, standing almost within singeing range of the first trailer, fists on hips, shaking his sandy head as if in disbelief. I ran towards him, the questions on my tongue clumsy, tripping over each other with urgent anxiety.

Before I reached him a hand reached out of the crowd and caught my arm, swinging me round, and it was Chris. There were smuts of smoke across his face, raw flesh in his palms. He was all right. I started to cry.

And then, between one sob and the next, while relief was still unlocking the tension in my diaphragm, my forearms and my scalp, I knew what I had done. My mouth dropped open and stayed open. Horror and guilt surged in me like a sickness. I had done the unthinkable, the unforgivable. I had escaped with my life, crawling on my belly through a choking cotton tunnel, and I had left the codex behind. I had left that beautiful, brilliant thing to burn.

If it was unthinkable it was certainly unspeakable. I could not tell Chris what I had done, though I was aware that he was staring into my face with growing concern, conscious that he was asking me questions though their meaning did not penetrate the shell of my shock. I was locked in a solitary confinement of the soul, with me and my crime on the inside and the rest of the world watching through the bars. Chris too belonged to that watching world, his anxious eyes innocent, his torn hands clean. I pushed him away.

I found myself backing numbly towards the fire. Those first few steps were entirely arbitrary, a matter only of putting distance between myself and those I had betrayed. But when I felt the heat at my back I turned, and I saw that the fire was still in the roof of the trailer, had yet to spread downwards. The codex in its leather drum was still safe on the seat where I left it, and for just a few minutes more might still be accessible.

The heat was fierce, but tenable to a soul already burning in another purgatory. I took my first deliberate step towards the trailer. Then I had my arms over my face and I was running towards it.

Again my brother's hand stopped me, the fingers digging like talons into the flesh of my arm. Without being told he knew – from my face, from my actions – the disaster which had befallen me. He shook his head and shouted above the bellow of the flames. 'It's too late.'

'No,' I cried foolish with desperation, 'there's still time.'

'It'll come down any moment.'

'I can't leave it. It's – priceless.'

'It's not worth your life.'

'I promised I'd guard it. I promised! I promised Richard – '

'Annie, this isn't your fault. Richard can't blame you for what's happened.'

But in my heart I knew he would, and that it would destroy him. That codex meant everything to him – for itself and for its implications for his reputation in a profession he held dear in a land he loved. I thought of that strange, bitter love, the intensity of his unreturned affection, and I believed that – one way or another, directly or indirectly, now or soon – the destruction of the codex would result in that of Richard Balfour. I couldn't bear that on my conscience. 'Chris, let me go.'

He shook his head and his grip was like iron.

In the bizarre intimacy of our exchange, shouted over the roar of the flames, cut off by crowds and incomprehension, neither of us saw Angel draw close, her narrow boyish head bent to follow our debate. Now she touched one hand to Chris's shoulder with the lightness of a moth's touch and said, just audibly, 'I'll get it.' She was away, a running figure string-thin against the bright flames, before either of us could react.

It was the first of three acts of memorable bravery which I witnessed that afternoon, distinct and separate acts though the chronology was such that they seemed to bleed together in a mounting crescendo of courage.

It was not, after all, as if Angel knew what was in the drum. The codex was a national treasure, a Mexican national treasure, and Angel and all her people would be the poorer for its loss. It was a thing beyond value, perhaps even worth a life, and if she had known about it perhaps I could have understood what she did. But she knew only that it was something of mine which I held dear, which I would have chanced my own life for but that I was prevented from doing so. It could have been anything: family photos, cocaine, money. It didn't matter. We had become friends, and it was in Angel's nature to risk herself for her friends. That was the first generous act of courage.

The second was when Chris, who had already given as much, mentally and physically, as he had to offer, found some remaining depth to plumb and dredged up enough strength to go after her. Dragging the overheated air into his lungs as a man might drag on whisky, he thrust me into powerful hands – Blair's, that gripped mostly out of surprise but held fast when he saw what was happening. Then he elbowed aside a couple of men who were staring after Angel and took off in her wake. He was clearly exhausted, running not on stamina but on sheer determination. But when a sudden gout of flame burst from the side of the trailer, roaring like a furnace, the girl broke her stride, staring in horror at where she was, and

Chris caught her. He grabbed her hand and spun her round, and flung her ahead of him back to the aghast and watching crowd.

And the blaze which had already eaten through the cargo ropes now ate away the timber shoring, and half the load came tumbling towards us in a sudden flaming avalanche. Angel missed being engulfed in it by inches. Chris disappeared under it.

It was then, stunned and reeling, screaming his name and knowing he was lost, that I witnessed the third and I still think the bravest of those three extraordinary acts of selflessness. Blair pressed me into other arms and ran to meet the fire, and he kicked and clawed at the burning bales, and tore his shirt off when it began to smoulder, until he got down to my brother's hand. Without pausing to investigate whether he was alive or dead, he grabbed the burnt hand and dragged him clear, and kept hauling him away from the flames until others came to help.

4

Under the clamour of the flames there was a stunned near-silence. Angel was softly sobbing; I was weeping soundlessly, the tears streaming down my face. Chris was crying too, whimpering gasps of pain he was too hurt to smother, not too shocked to feel. Blair had got to him in time to save his life but too late to prevent widespread damage. Deep burns, blackened with the charred fibres of cotton and his clothing driven into them, covered the backs of his hands and arms, thrown up to shield his head, and spread across his shoulders. Another flaming bale had burst over his legs: his jeans were burnt away and his skin seared from mid-thigh to calf down the back of his right leg, only a little less on his left.

Incredibly, although not without reason, I found myself wrestling with the mathematics of his injuries. Two factors

152

govern the severity of burns: depth, and the proportion of body area affected. I had no way of judging the first, so it seemed important to me to be accurate and objective about the second. I settled on fifteen percent. That wasn't too bad, was it? Rummaging through an attic of memories, I felt sure I'd heard of people making good recoveries from much more extensive burning. Of course, they mostly had one thing in common: swift and professional medical treatment.

I looked up and found Blair bending over us. There were glistening red marks on his arms where his shirt had burned but he seemed unaware of them, at least for the moment. The ruined shirt he had pulled back on just as soon as they were both safe, like an ant washing its antennae.

I said, 'You have to get him to a hospital.'

He avoided my eyes. 'I can't.'

'He needs a doctor. You have to get him to a hospital. Now, damn you!'

'I can't. How can I? My rig's burnt out and I've got forty prospective wetbacks to move out of here before the Policía move in. You want me to make a detour round the local hospital? We're all going to end up in jail, lady.'

We were very close, conversing in an angry sotto voce, eyeball to eyeball as we leaned together over Chris's ravaged back. It was no distance for me to reach and take hold of Blair's shirt-front. Had I tried it standing up it would have looked absurd; kneeling, we were more nearly the same height and the gesture seemed, to me and somehow also to him, a legitimate way of lending emphasis to my words. If we looked a little like a rat shaking a terrier, it didn't occur to either of us just then.

With quiet fury I said, 'This kid's in the state he's in because of your basic inability to organise a piss-up in a brewery. I agreed to come on this trip because I was told it would be safe, for me and also for the article I was carrying. Well, that article is now cinders, and I would

have been too, and so would all these people, except for
him. He told you what was going to happen. You wouldn't
have it. And even when it happened and the thing was on
fire, you didn't bloody notice until he clawed his way up
the side of the truck to tell you!'

Blair said, 'I noticed.'

'What?'

'I saw the fire – before you did, I reckon. I was looking
for some place to get off the road.'

'We were burning in there!'

'No, you weren't. Nobody was hurt until you decided to
go back for that thing. And nobody would have been hurt
if you'd had the sense to bring it with you when you got
out.'

It was true. It was absolutely true, but it wasn't what I
wanted to hear. I didn't need Blair or anyone to point out
my culpability when guilt was like a sharp knife under my
ribs that twisted with every whine of agony my brother
couldn't help uttering. I needed help, not more grief.

I put his shirt down. 'Look at him. Are you going to let
him suffer like that?'

'No.' Blair stood up, big against the flames, and walked
away. He opened the door of the cab – the first thing they
had done, before coming to free us, was disengage the
tractor and drive it a safe distance from the blazing load –
and climbed up. For a dreadful moment I thought he had
gone for a gun.

He came back with a syringe. It may have been
morphine from his first-aid kit; I think it was heroin. 'No,
that is something I can do something about.'

He had difficulty finding firm, undamaged flesh for the
injection. Burns covered the obvious areas of both arms.
After a moment, handing me the syringe to hold, he
worked his fingers into the burnt hole in Chris's jeans and
tore the fabric upwards, exposing enough unblackened
skin to sink the needle.

Coursing through other veins the stuff was mayhem. In

his, then, it was respite from appalling pain that spread rapidly, easing his tortured breathing, quieting his cries, unlocking the terrible rigidity his body had adopted in the desperate search for relief. He didn't lose consciousness but lapsed quickly into a trancelike gentleness, apparently aware of what was happening around him without making any attempt to react. The knotted muscles of his face relaxed with those of his body, the harsh lines blurring. His eyes softened and deepened, the lids sliding to half-mast. He mumbled something. I bent my head low over his face and he mumbled again but I still didn't understand him. I saw tears on his cheek and thought for a moment they were his, but they were mine.

Blair had gone back to the cab for a blanket – the distances involved in pan-American trucking require two drivers, a bunk and a shift system. When Chris was safe from the pain Blair spread the blanket over him, wrapping him carefully, and picked him up. He carried him to the cab slung over his shoulder like a roll of carpet. It looked terribly casual: in fact it was as good a way of keeping pressure off his burns as could have been improvised.

When he was settled in the bunk, quiet and withdrawn, watching ambivalently with glassy half-hooded eyes, Blair took me aside with one long arm around my shoulders while his colleagues shooed our fellow-travellers away.

'OK,' he said, 'This is what we're going to do. You, me and the truck are getting out of here now. The rest of them can split up and never be noticed, they can try again next week or next month; same goes for my crew. But if you, me or this' – a thumb over his shoulder at the cab, looming somehow bigger than ever in splendid isolation, stripped of its trailers – 'get picked up we're going to be answering questions right up to the time they slam the door and throw away the key. We'll get off the road, travel across country. We'll take the kid with us. Once we're well away from here we'll leave him somewhere they can get him to a doctor.'

I frowned, trying to make sense of what he was saying. Partly it was my understanding that was working on three cylinders, but partly I was aware that there were things he was not saying. 'Why not leave him here?'

'For the cops? They find him here, they know what he's part of. The fact he's hurt won't stop them asking him the same questions, and – ' He stopped abruptly, evidently thinking better of what he had been about to say.

'And?' I waited.

He looked past my shoulder, at the wreck of the trailer, still burning though not with the same vigour. 'And they may want answers before they'll let the doctors have him. That shot I gave him won't last forever.'

I had no way of knowing if the Mexican police did behave that way or if his way of life filled his mind with neurotic spectres. But I believed Blair thought it a serious possibility. It was the sort of treatment he expected if he fell into their hands. I didn't think – fresh from my safe Welsh home, my mother's house, the good job in my other brother's school, with no clouds to threaten beyond the first period with 3b on April Fool's Day – that it could happen. But I couldn't be sure.

'All right. Drive us ten miles up the road and leave us somewhere I can get him to a hospital. I'll take it from there.'

His eyes flared whitely. 'You? No way, lady. You're coming with me. Somebody has to explain to our mutual friend what happened to his latest toy, and it sure as hell isn't going to be me.'

My heart pounded. 'What are you suggesting – that we dump him by the roadside somewhere? He might not be found for hours. He'd be better off with the police.'

He breathed heavily at me. I think he was finding me hard work. 'A gas station. That suit you, lady, we leave him at a gas station? They'll have a phone and they'll have transport. They'll see him OK.'

They would also have eyes, and know one truck from

another, and be likely to notice registration numbers. 'At a gas station?'

His eyes shifted. 'Well, near a gas station.'

If we'd still been on our knees I'd have taken a swing at him. 'Get this straight, Blair. I'm not leaving him. Unless I can leave him with someone I trust, I'm not leaving him at all. If that means taking my chances with the police, so be it. I owe him, and I'm not leaving him in a ditch on the off-chance that some peasant may eventually come along on a donkey.' A sudden sob came up and I choked it. 'We haven't even the time to be arguing like this. He should be on his way to a hospital *now*!'

I don't know how it would have ended. Clearly Blair could have ended it right there with a sharp right hook and me too draped over his shoulder. Perhaps he was too unsure of my relationship with his boss to take that option, at least while others remained. I wouldn't have backed down over Chris, have left him to fend for himself with injuries like his, so probably it would have come to blows.

Again it was Angel who came out for her friends. I found her standing behind me, tall and thin as willow, the flamboyance of her clothes spoiled by dust and ash. Her face was tear-stained but she was not crying now. 'You need someone to stay with him?' It was only partly a question; mostly it was a statement of fact, and also of intent. 'I'll stay.'

I turned and looked up at her, my heart brimming with thanks even as my common sense rejected it. 'Angel, you can't. No little country doctor is going to deal with burns like that. It'll be a hospital, and when the police find this lot the first thing they'll do is drag the hospitals for fresh burns. They'll certainly find him, and if you're with him they'll find you too.'

'I know.'

She did. And I knew she did. 'What about America? What about your savings? It was all for nothing if you stay behind now.'

'I'll get to America sometime. I can always make more money. I don't care about the money. Your friend got hurt saving my ass, and anything I can do to help I want to do. Policía?' She suddenly grinned and snapped her fingers. 'How the hell you think I make a living if I can't handle Policía?'

The offer was like a weight lifted from my soul. It left room for anger. 'It shouldn't be down to you, it's down to me. He's my' – I remembered in time, just – 'employee. What happened to him is my fault, getting him fixed up is my responsibility. I can look after him. There's no point in me going on. If I get any hassle from the police I can go to the British consul, and when I'm ready to leave I can do it on my British passport. Blair, this is crazy – '

'I told you,' he said, cutting in with a sharpness that somehow suggested unease more than it did impatience. It was the only time I detected anything approaching fear in him. 'I'm not going back without you. If Miss Mendoza' – I hadn't until that moment known or wondered about her second name – 'is prepared to stay with him, that should set your mind at rest. And I'll make sure, Miss Mendoza, when you're ready to leave you'll be on the first run and it won't cost you nothing.'

Actually I could do better for her than that, if she'd only believe and trust me without asking how.

'All right,' I said, wearily. 'OK, you win. But by God, Blair, you'd better honour that promise.'

'Lady, you're in no position to make threats,' he said heavily.

Privately I thought he was probably right, but the thing had not yet taken its last silly twist. As the three of us moved towards the cab, ready to drive away and leave the rest to shift as best they might, the boy Juliano approached, diffidently, something blackened and malformed in his hands. He held it out to me. It was the leather drum, burnt and twisted but still somehow intact, the lid in place. He rattled out an explanation.

Angel translated, her voice numb, aware that this was what she had risked her life for and why Chris had almost lost his. 'He says, when the cotton fell down this came with it. When the fire died back he pulled it out.'

I took it from him and said, very quietly, '*Gracias*.' I had no idea what it contained, from a slightly battered codex to a pile of chalky fragments. I didn't want to know.

Blair said, 'Aren't you going to open it?' His voice was a reverent whisper.

I looked at him as a man eating an apple might view half a worm. 'Are you mad? If by the grace of God there is anything in here worth having, it's going to need stabilising, rehydrating, the surface will have to be sealed and heaven knows what else.' I was making it up as I went along, more or less, but Blair didn't know that. If there's one thing a teacher learns it's how to sound authoritative on a subject of which she knows next to nothing. 'If that lid comes off now, I can just about guarantee we'll lose it. In a controlled environment, preferably a laboratory, with tools and baths and chemicals, maybe we'll save it. I don't know. But I'm not pre-empting that possibility. Do you want to?'

He said nothing. He turned away and climbed up into the truck, and after a moment the engine thundered into life.

I seized the scant privacy it gave us and caught Angel's arm with my free hand. 'Listen. Say nothing. When we leave you, get him to the nearest hospital and stay there. Stay there! I'll come back for you. Tell the police everything but don't leave. Wait for me.'

She looked at me, then her gaze travelled to the cab – seeing not Blair at the wheel but the hidden figure in the cot, wrapped in a blanket, vacant-eyed with narcotics, mumbling with the memory of pain. She said softly, '*Migras*?'

I didn't know the word. I shrugged. She smiled and nodded slightly. '*Migras*.'

She went to the cab and climbed up beside Blair, and I

didn't for the life of me know if I'd blown it and whether either Chris or I had any future to look forward to. I had asked Angel to trust me with her freedom, unquestioning, without reason or explanation. Walking to the cab with my charred burden, I was aware that by doing so I had trusted her with my life and my brother's.

I wished to God I knew what *Migras* were.

We left the devastation behind. Blair drove for maybe forty minutes, heading due north up a good road. For the first time I could see the names on the signs, names that meant nothing to me then but would later: Oballos, El Sauz, Sabinas, Nueva Rosita, Palau, Zaragoza. Nuevo Laredo I knew, but there were still a lot of kilometres before that one. But the names and the signs and something in the blood told me we were approaching if not actually entering the border area. Allusions, when they came, to the Rio Bravo del Norte fooled me not at all. The Rio Grande by any other name would still be the US border.

Angel rode beside Blair in the cab and for the most part I squatted in a few square feet beside the cot. It suited Blair – there was nothing memorable about an American trucker and a Mexican girl, whereas the three of us might upset the balance of the thing enough to be noticed – and it suited me because I could monitor my brother's condition without constantly being seen to do so.

Not that I learnt anything helpful. I didn't know enough to judge whether he was doing well or dying. His pulse seemed light and quick but steady enough; his skin was cool and clammy with a dew of sweat. Cocooned in narcosis, he hovered between awareness and oblivion, neither wholly conscious nor sleeping. He seemed to watch me from a great distance. I couldn't tell if he was still hurting, if the drug had killed the pain or just deadened his ability to communicate it: muffled only the screams, not the desire to scream. I didn't disturb the blanket, I knew there was nothing I could do about what lay beneath. Mostly I just held his hand – carefully, from underneath, avoiding the burns along the back – and stroked his hair, and hoped he found more comfort in these gestures than I did, and counted the miles and the bumps in the road.

Several times in those forty minutes, again across the great void that seemed to yawn between his injured body and his floating mind, he tried to say something to me, but only once was I able to make any sense of it. I think he was just beginning to come back from wherever the drugs had taken him. He knew it was me sitting cramped there beside him; his fingers tightened fractionally on mine and he said my name.

In reply I said something predictable and inane: 'Lie still now' or 'You're all right' or 'Everything's going to be OK'. It wasn't good enough for him. He was fighting his way back to awareness, battling his body's need for sleep, focusing his eyes by willpower alone. Again he stumbled out my name, urgency a rough burr in his voice.

I leaned low over him. 'What is it, Chris?'

Agitation was rough in his throat like gravel. 'Don't care,' he breathed, enunciating clearly through the cotton wool crowding his brain. 'You don't care.'

At first, shocked and hurt, I thought it was an accusation and rocked back on my heels. Then I realised what he was saying. This far on – this hurt, this weak, this tormented – he was still looking out for me. With his senses wrapped in pain and seductive lunacy, he could still perceive more clearly than I the danger to which I would expose us if I appeared to care too much about what happened to him. He was hired help, a friend's friend. It was one thing to be shocked at the episode, horrified at its outcome. But it mustn't be personal. I mustn't care. If Blair caught me caring, questions would be asked that I couldn't answer.

I squeezed his fingers and straightened up. I said plaintively, 'Blair, if we don't get rid of this kid soon we're going to be carting a body round.' I felt a faint answering pressure on my hand and I swear that as he let his eyes close my brother smiled.

'We're nearly there,' said Blair.

We had come through the place called Nueva Rosita and were heading away on the north-bound highway. I looked ahead, between his head and Angel's. There wasn't much to see, only the usual jumble of industrial flotsam that lines the high-water mark of any urban area, most of it connected in one way or another with the business of the road. There was plenty of other traffic around, much of it obviously local, some of it big rigs like ours going international. If we were hoping to pass unnoticed as we dropped off a young girl and an injured man, I doubted if we were in the right place.

But Blair knew where he was, all right. He found a sliproad on the left, and off it to the right an even narrower track, and where we stopped there was a corrugated iron fence between us and traffic we could hear but not see. The big airbrakes hissed on but he didn't turn the engine off. We weren't staying that long.

He hefted Chris out of the cot and through the cab, probably being as careful as he could but relying pretty heavily on the drug circulating in his bloodstream to soften the edges of the furniture and the hardness of his hands. He knelt and laid the injured man on his face beside the fence. The bright sun was overhead and there was no shade, but the afternoon was cooler than it had looked through the windscreen. Only two hundred miles north there might still be the residue of that improbable snowfall on the high desert hills.

Blair straightened up, turned to Angel. 'When we're gone, follow this fence round and you'll find a gas station. There's a phone there. Call the nearest hospital and tell them – oh, tell them he was crushed, he was changing a wheel and the car fell on him. Don't mention burns. It don't matter that as soon as they see him they're going to know different: point is, he'll be in hospital before the cops turn up. If you say he's burned the cops'll turn up first.'

He reached back into the cab. 'You'll need these.' One was a thick wad of money, I couldn't guess how much but it looked a substantial amount. I didn't think Blair was giving his own money away: it was probably Rivera's. The other was a charged syringe. 'Give him another shot if the pain gets bad before the medics get here. And give it him if you think the cops are coming. But don't let them catch you with it.'

That was it. He climbed back into the cab.

I held her hands a moment. I wanted to cry. 'Thanks, Angel. For everything. Look after him, but look after yourself too. I'll be in touch. Make sure I can find you.'

Blair was gunning the engine. We embraced briefly and I turned away and left them there. I had no idea if I would see either of them again.

Blair drove back on to the northbound road, for only half a mile. Then we left it again, heading almost due west, the sun in our eyes. Rough ground thundered up at us through the wheels. Sometimes we were on tarmac, sometimes on dirt road, sometimes he seemed to be plotting a compass course across virgin land. The land was a wilderness, marginally desert, brakes of shaly sand twining fingers with brakes of tough greening thorn and the occasional cactus. Always, whichever way you looked, there were mountains to fret the skyline. It was a hard, harsh landscape – at least until the rains would bring a softening of colour and the ultimate transcience of petals to dance on the desert wind – but it had its beauty too. When the sun went down the sky went the colour of apricots and the mountains turned from blue to soft smoky grey.

We crossed a river, joined a half-decent road, left it again. The sun was a copper ball full in our faces. If Angel had told the police we were driving north, they would do an awful lot of looking before they found us.

We travelled like that for the guts of eight hours. We saw hardly a handful of people. Twice the track we were on

headed towards a village, and Blair drove off into the
desert rather than risk being seen. Then there were no
more roads, no villages, no people. It occurred to me that
if Blair had decided to kill me it would be here, and no one
would ever know or even guess to within a hundred miles.
But he just kept driving, his eyes scanning out mule-tracks
and goat-tracks that most mules and goats would have
given up on, the wheel of the high tractor bucking in his
hands.

Even when it went dark he didn't stop. Headlamps like
searchlights sprang out, and he picked his way from one
landmark to another by a combination of sight, feel and
intuition. He had clearly been this way before and knew
how the land lay. From time to time he would grunt a quiet
satisfaction when what he was watching for appeared in
the raking headlights: a ridge, an arroyo, a certain gnarled
and scrubby little tree. Mostly these heralded a change of
direction but always the general bearing was northwest
backing north. If we turned much from that heading it was
to avoid something impassable, and we always returned
when the obstacle was passed.

We crossed another river – broader than the first, almost
too broad it seemed for the amount of water in it. Driving
up the far bank Blair said, 'Welcome to the United States.'

I twisted in my seat and stared back but there was
nothing to see. 'That was the border?' He nodded. 'Then
we're in the clear?'

He took his eyes off the hill we were scaling, just for a
moment, and looked at me as if I were mad. 'Jesus, lady,
you don't know much about this, do you?'

'Blair,' I said, willing him to believe me, 'I don't know
anything about this. I know something about Mexican
history, I know something about archaeological artifacts.
That's how I got here: doing someone a favour. I thought
it would be like – oh, like bringing an extra bottle of
burgundy through the green channel at Customs. I didn't
expect all this. I didn't expect anyone to get hurt.'

'People get hurt all the time,' he replied, obliquely. 'You want things, you've got to take risks. The greasers know that.'

I knew it too. I couldn't even say I hadn't been warned. But the reality had come as a shock. I had spent too long in classrooms. Half of me craved the comfortable familiarity of 3b and the traditional Monday-morning bawling out. Yet the other half knew even now, anxious and apprehensive as I was, numb with weariness and dull with fear, that I wouldn't go back, that it would never again be enough for me. To go back would be to live in a dream, remembering the reality of struggling for survival among these blue and brown hills until the contrast – the contrast, not the memory – became too painful. I didn't know where my future lay – I wasn't yet counting on having one – but I would have to find one that was more than teaching history to Welsh schoolboys primarily to keep them off the rugby pitch long enough for the groundsman to get round with the limewash.

At the same time, I could live on a lot less excitement than I'd had this past week.

Blair said, out of nowhere, 'You want some advice?'

I looked at him. 'Probably.'

We were on a sort of road for the present, but he still didn't lift his eyes from the pool of the headlights. 'If this – codex? – of yours really is ruined, you want to have something else ready to offer him. He can be tricky when he's mad.'

I shrugged. 'Mason? It's not Mason that concerns me. If it's not worth having he won't buy it, it's as simple as that. What worries me is having to explain to Richard how he hasn't the money he needs to get out of the country and the codex is gone. I don't know what he'll do.'

'It sounds like he'll go to jail,' said Blair, with heavy humour. 'Unless you want a piece of that, you'd better tell him long distance.'

There was another fairly lengthy pause, but he hadn't

finished. He came back to the subject. 'Listen, Miss Meredith, I don't need to go out on a limb talking to you this way. I'm in trouble too: I've lost him a rig, a cargo, and a bunch of greasers he'd have got a premium from supplying as labour. The codex too – even though you left it in there, he's going to blame me for the fire. So I don't need to take any risks just now.

'But I've weathered problems before and I'll weather this one, because I'm useful to him. I run this operation for him better than anyone else could – better than he could himself, even if he was willing to take the risks, which he isn't. So he needs me. He'll shout – kind of quiet, you ever hear anyone shouting under their breath? – and he'll threaten me, but in the end he'll accept what happened as an occupational hazard because he needs what I give him. It's an edge. That's what you're going to need.'

An edge? The only edge I'd ever had was the edge of my tongue. And some money, but not the kind that would impress a man like Mason. All I had was the codex, or what was left of it inside that charred and twisted drum. Instinctively I hugged it to me. I was sorry about what had happened to it – sorry for Richard, sorry for Alvarado, sorry for the Mexican people who had lost a great treasure. But mostly I was sorry for myself, because it had been my passport to safety, and if I had come to the conclusion that a body could be too safe, I had by no means forgotten how much worse it was not to be safe enough. My mind wrestled with the problem while Blair wrestled with the wheel. If he had met with the same success we should have ended upside down in a gully.

Finally we seemed to drive up the almost sheer side of a mountain, and when we paused on the summit there were lights in the blackness below: a cluster of bright pinpoints that were too few for a town, too many for a house – at least, most houses.

'Sugar Valley?'

Blair nodded.

We had come over the ring of rock encircling the valley, over the high rim at which I had gazed up. The lights were burning late in the Mason house, and in the small settlement of barns, yards and living quarters that served it. Perhaps, at midnight, it was too early to say that Mason was waiting up for us, but one of the crewmen left behind would have called him, and if Blair knew this overland route so well it seemed likely that either his colleagues or his employer would know how long it took. The lights were for us, to guide us in off the mountain.

We came down like a stooping eagle, near enough vertically and at speed. The track was straight now and stayed in our headlights, and Blair responded – after eight hours crouched over the wheel, picking his way from one rock to the next – by opening the throttle and shrugging off the brake. He grinned at me, his broad angular face ghostly in the backwash of light from the instruments, and that grin was the only thing between me and screaming terror, because all my instincts told me that no sane man drives like that down a mountain in the dark. As it was I wedged my feet among the furniture; if I had been any more scared I think I'd have taken my chances going out the side exit.

But he knew what he was doing, as he had known all along, and when the path began to flatten he eased back on the big engine and we trundled the last half-mile down to the house and pulled up in front of the wide sweeping steps. If the juxtaposition of desert-stained truck with gracious hacienda seemed incongruous, there was no one to notice the irony who didn't already have weightier matters on his mind.

Before the great engine had choked to a guttering silence the double doors at the top of the steps had been thrown wide and Raoul Mason was advancing to meet us. Blair and I exchanged a last glance and got down on either side of the cab, and waited.

5

Despite his age and that slight, interesting air of frailty that was more suggested than specified, Mason was taking the steps two at a time in his haste to reach us. It boded ill that a man who had invested so much in his own dignity should be so agitated as to abandon it. He'd heard, and he hadn't liked what he'd heard.

When he came up to us he demanded of Blair, 'What happened?' and of me, 'Is it safe?' and the questions came out like machine-gun fire, so quick I could not afterwards be sure which came first.

Blair said, 'The cotton I picked up in Pachuca must have been wet. It went up.'

I said, 'Raoul, I honest to God don't know.' I held out the drum. He looked with horror at its cracked and flaking skin, its twisted lines. His hands recoiled from taking it. With a jerk of his head he beckoned us inside.

In my ignorance I wondered whether Blair, as a hired man, would have been inside the house before. But at the top of the steps he took the lead, crossing the great atrium hall, turning right through the conservatory to the private study where I had been entertained by Raoul Mason the first night we met.

It occurred to me, following, Mason stalking grimly at my side, that I had finally established the link – the connection between the two men which had always been suspected and never before proven, the link which would put the rich and ruthless Frenchman behind bars for a very long time. For a moment I couldn't understand why I wasn't more pleased to have achieved what I had come here for.

But both the ground-rules and the stakes had changed

since I came into the game. I had embarked in a spirit of anger and grief to avenge a brother it now transpired wasn't dead. I had indeed acquired the evidence I had sought – of one murder, the Colombian's, if not those of the six men dead in an abandoned trailer in the cold high hills. Unfortunately, I found myself in the situation facing so many eye-witnesses: the man I could testify against knew it, and when he saw what I had done to his coveted codex he was just likely to decide that the risks of having me around outweighed the benefits. I knew, now, he was a man who was prepared to kill to protect himself. It seemed on the cards that, to protect himself, he would be prepared to kill me.

Blair was right. What I needed was an edge, something I could offer to rebalance the scales. I couldn't think of a single god-damned thing.

Blair might be familiar with his employer's home, but not to the point of contempt. Once in the study he stayed on his feet, awkward and tall among the comfortable chairs, waiting to be told to sit. No such niceties troubled me: I was older than him, I was female, and all I'd had out of Mason's wallet was supper and an air excursion to Mexico City. I flopped on the settee where we had sat together and talked, and I put the leather drum in front of me on the table where we had served ourselves from the bottle of wine. All our eyes watched it, as if it might do something.

At length Mason took a seat, waved Blair perfunctorily to another. Without moving his eyes he said tersely, 'Blair, what happened?'

Blair told him – everything, in detail. He told him about the fire: how Chris had raised the alarm, how in the evacuation I had forgotten the codex, how Angel had gone back for it and Chris had gone after her. The only detail he omitted was how he came by his own injuries.

Mason turned eyes on me like slow fire. 'You left *that* to burn?' There was madness in his voice like blood in his throat, but his voice was low – low enough it was some effort to hear him. He was shouting under his breath.

I flared my nostrils at him, summoning up anger. 'You're damn right I did. That place was a death-trap. It could have killed us all at any moment.'

'But it didn't.'

'A minute later it came down all over the place. No one would have got out. Only two people were within fifty feet of it: the girl was lucky, the boy's in a Mexican hospital with half his back burned away.' My eyes caught Blair's. 'He was pretty lucky, too, even at that.'

'You think I care,' murmured Mason, his voice dropping ever lower, 'how many Mexicans there are in the world – even to the nearest million? That artifact was unique. It was priceless, irreplaceable. There will never be another like it. There may never be another found. Your carelessness is unforgivable.' I detected a tremor in his words that at first I ascribed to the unnatural depth of his register. Then I saw it was a reflection of a visible tremble in his hands and his knees. The man was literally shaking with fury.

Once, years ago, I read somewhere that attack is the best means of defence. It might be an exaggeration to say I founded my entire life on that philosophy, but if I sued for slander the damages wouldn't buy my bus-fare home. I felt the expected surge of adrenalin hammer through the fear; nurturing it, I leaned right forward in my seat and pointed my finger up his nose.

'Listen, sonny,' I spat, for all the world as if he were the Al Capone of 3b, 'I have news for you. I too am unique and irreplaceable. I don't have to be here. I didn't have to do this. I risked my liberty, and as it turns out my life, not for my benefit but for yours and for my friend's. And he treated me as if I was trying to rob him at that end, and you're treating me like I burst your balloon at this. Raoul, after the day I've had, I don't need any of this.

'And that's another thing,' I went on, warming to the

subject. 'You said I would be safe. You said you could make sure I was safe. I have to tell you, locked inside a funeral pyre doing fifty on the open road, I did not feel safe. You want to know who's responsible for the state of that codex? You are – you and the people you trusted implicitly to look after me, who couldn't even tell wet cotton from dry cotton, and didn't even know what it meant when the difference was pointed out. Professionals? They're about as much use as roller-skates to a steeplejack.'

From the look on his face, no one had spoken to Raoul Mason that way in a very long time. From the look on *his* face, Blair had sometimes wondered what would happen if anyone did. There was a stillness and a quiet in the scholarly little room, as if we were all three of us waiting to find out.

For long seconds Mason's eyes lay on me like coals, hot and full of power, until my cheeks flushed and I began to imagine spots of burning. Then he turned slowly in his seat and his gaze swivelled to Blair. 'She has a point.'

However confident he was in his usefulness and the ability that gave him to weather whatever storms arose, Blair still stiffened under that brutal gaze. 'She has indeed,' he agreed. 'Gallegos sold me a bad load, and when the mess is cleaned up I mean to pay him a visit to express our disappointment. We were lucky: nobody got killed, the truck wasn't stopped, nobody we left behind can lead the cops here, and we got the cab home. It could have been a lot worse. I don't want it happening again.'

'Again?' whispered Mason. '*Again*? You'll never carry a load this precious again as long as you live.'

We were back to the codex. That meant we were back to me. The gaze was slowly swivelling my way again when I said, 'Listen, we're all upset. And tired. Maybe we're jumping to conclusions. That case was made to protect it. It's still more or less intact. Maybe the codex is too.'

More of those long seconds passed while we looked at the scorched and twisted tube. I didn't believe it. I couldn't tell what the others believed.

Finally Blair said, 'You said you couldn't open it.' Tones of hope and accusation warred in his voice.

'By a Mexican roadside, with the wind full of dust and ash? You're damn right I wasn't going to open it there. I don't even think we should open it here. Raoul, do you have a laboratory anywhere?' With his business interests, at least some of his money had to be in the Texas oil patch and that meant laboratories. So did chemicals, or medicine, or photography – My heart skipped a beat. That was a possibility that I hadn't considered: that he might have a darkroom here in the house, in which case I would gain neither time nor the involvement of other people.

He hadn't. And whatever patience he had he'd used up as well. 'There's no wind in here.'

I tried desperately to remember the line I'd spun Blair. 'You've got polymer stabilisers, have you? Clear emulsions? Hydrologised proteins?' I think I got that off the back of a cornflakes packet. 'If the surface has separated, you know and I know there's nothing we can do about it on your desk with the contents of your Little Businessman pencil-case.'

'If the surface has separated?' Perhaps because they don't go in for riches and property, and therefore manage to avoid the worst effects of megalomania, even when they're thwarted you don't often hear such venom hissing from real snakes. 'If the surface has separated there's nothing worth having. It's destroyed.'

'Not necessarily ... ' The most important department of any museum, after the accountants whose job is getting grants out of government, is the conservation branch. What's in the glass cases is for show, and it's certainly very nice to have one of the three surviving golden chamberpots from the winter palace of King Olav the Incontinent, but the work of the museum is complete before the general public get clapping its nasty common ignorant little eyes on the stuff. The real work is done on site, because archaeological context is all, and then in the museum workshops where conservationists reconstruct, stabilise, preserve and protect anachronistic survivors which should have rotted away with the rest of their culture centuries or millennia ago and now, freed from the time capsule, set about doing it as fast as they can before your very eyes. Almost nothing you see in a museum is as it was when it was found. You owe the fact that it tells you something about itself and its makers to the skill of the conservers.

'Miss Meredith, I am a collector. Not a scientist, not an historian – a collector. I buy beautiful things for pleasure. I have no time for significant fragments, deeply important dregs. I want things I can display, things I can look at. That was what you promised me: an incomplete but essentially intact Mixtec codex, a composition of pictures in pigment on a prepared deerhide. A thing you could mount, light and take pride in displaying. A thing whose beauty is not dependent on the specialist knowledge of the beholder.

'That is what you promised me; that's all I'm interested in. If I take the top off this drum and find that what you have brought me is a million-piece jigsaw of coloured pieces and plain pieces, I shall flush them down the tubes. And then I shall do much the same with you.'

It was a real threat, not rhetoric, I could tell by the coldness that had leached in behind the hot coals of his eyes, but still my heart leapt first for the codex. 'You can't do that! Whatever state it's in, that thing is priceless. Maybe we can't reconstruct it, but any decent museum could. Even if they can't restore the pictures, there's so much they can learn from trying. You can't destroy something that rare. Even if it's no use to you, you must see how important it is to archaeology?'

His eyes were now quite cold and his voice was bleak. 'That does not concern me.' He reached out with hands that were almost steady and picked up the leather drum, and took the lid off.

For an age of moments he stared into it, the angle such that neither Blair nor I could share his view. Blair was watching his face. I was watching his right hand, the hand that had removed the lid and which now lay as if abandoned in his lap. If there was anything there to take out, that right hand would do it. Movement there would be the first sign I would see that my error had not been a fatal one, that I still had something to buy my safety with.

For a split second I thought I saw that movement, but it was the muscles of his fist clenching. Then without taking his right hand from his lap, his left held the drum out over the coffee table and, quite slowly, turned it upside down.

And fragments of colour, and fragments of white, and tiny shrivelled scraps of deerhide hardly heavier than the tense air in the little room, fluttered out in a dense rainbow cloud that spread and fell slowly, like a child's snowstorm toy, and took minutes to settle in a thick mosaic like confetti on the glass top.

Blair, who had seen it in its glory, was clearly appalled. What I felt veered between grief and fear in a wild and terrible oscillation. And Mason? There seemed no way of knowing what he felt. He had gone quiet enough to be very, very dangerous. He leaned over, without speaking, and put the drum down, carefully, without dislodging the field of colours. Just the way he leaned, he put it down in front of Blair. He could as easily have put it in front of me, in which case things would have gone differently.

Somebody had to say something sometime. Finally, as the silence stretched and crawled, I said, 'You have no right – '

It was like pulling the plug on Boulder Dam. You can't very well shout sitting down, even quietly, so he stood up. He wasn't a big man in any physical sense, but he loomed then.

'Rights? You talk to me about rights? I had the right to expect you would fulfil your side of the bargain. You promised me a codex; you promised!' He was like a child in the candyfloss queue when the sugar runs out. His childlike perspective, his absolute lack of any sense of proportion, was frightening in a grown man – more deeply disturbing than his threats. 'I put my organisation, my own safety, at risk for it. You think it's my normal practice to tell young women I don't know from Eve that I have an operation capable of smuggling people and merchandise across the Mexican border? You think I got old and rich by doing that?

'Jesus God,' he went on, and the volume was mounting now, the veins standing proud and dark on his classical forehead, 'you're not even some hooker I don't know. You're the half-sister of a half-bred Fed – apart from my family, the only people you know in this country are Feds. You think you're going to walk out of here to tell them about me?'

Someone said, 'You knew who I was. You invited me here because of it.' I gathered it had to be me. Oddly, she sounded almost calm.

'That's right, I knew exactly who you were. I had my reasons for seeing you. But when you came up with this sob-story, I was ready to take a risk on you – for the codex, and because once you'd brought me that there was no way you could go back to your brother's friends. That is no longer the situation. There is no codex. You have destroyed it – murdered it. I don't have it, and there's no evidence that you brought it here. There's no evidence that you ever came here.'

'Raoul –!'

'Think about it. You're in Mexico City with my daughter. When she reports you missing that's where they'll look. It's a big country, a lot happens there that never comes to light. Nobody will be too surprised that you don't turn up. Except I think eventually you will, weeks or months from now, rotting in a roadside ditch. If I can smuggle live bodies one way, I can sure as hell smuggle a dead one the other.'

'Forty people on that rig know I came with Blair.'

'Yes, but they don't know Blair came to me. And nobody knows about them, who they are or where to start looking for them. They're not going to come forward to check on your well-being.'

He was right. Nobody could show that I'd ever returned to the States. Chris, if he recovered, would know, and might succeed in finding Blair – but only Blair, and only if Blair didn't find him first.

Almost as if the bloody man was a mind-reader, Blair said, 'There's the boy in the hospital.' He was turning the leather drum in his hands.

Mason nodded thoughtfully, quite sane again. 'Yes, we shall have to take care of him. And the girl with him as well.'

They were talking about killing us – me, and Chris, and poor Angel who'd had some bad luck in her life but nothing to compare with the day she fell in with me. They were discussing it as if I weren't there, evidence if any was still needed that they were absolutely serious, and I couldn't seem to stop them. Not even that, I couldn't seem to make any sound or gesture or words or crying to interrupt their discussion, even temporarily. I can't explain that. It must have seemed to them that either I didn't understand what they were saying or that somehow I was past caring.

In fact I understood perfectly and cared very much. The closest I can say it, all my mental energies were running along intellectual channels, leaving the emotional ones dry. I was looking for a key to the maze. I think by then I had known for some time that a cry for mercy, an appeal to the better nature of Raoul Mason, would achieve nothing beyond the further demoralisation of being laughed at. I was thinking for my life.

An edge, Blair had said. I needed an edge: something I could offer him that he had a use for. Something to buy back my life with. There was nothing. Well no, there was something, perhaps, but I was damned if I was selling.

Blair was still working on his clairvoyant act. He caught

my eye and, his brow faintly furrowed, transmitted a question-mark. I responded with the least perceptible shake of the head. He knew I had something. He couldn't believe I wouldn't trade.

And maybe after all it was safe to. Chris should have been in hospital seven hours by now, his injuries treated, his pain deadened. If he was conscious he would undoubtedly have got messages to the Policía and to Joshua Cade. Not only would he and Angel be safe, but help would be on its way to me right now, all I had to do was hang on until it arrived. Certainly if I started telling Mason that my brother had survived the death-trap in the hills and had infiltrated his organisation again, that he had talked with his mules and his customers and logged his staging posts across six hundred mountain miles from Mexico City to Nueva Rosita, and was now comfortable in a Mexican hospital chatting to the local police in person and the US police by phone, he would not have killed me until I had finished.

But that depended on assumptions I had no right to make. Last time I had seen him Chris hadn't been up to making detailed and complex explanations to policemen. He had been pretty well out of his mind with pain and drugs, and if Angel had given him the second shot, or if the hospital used something else on him, it could be hours yet before he started making sense. In those hours he would be terribly vulnerable. Hospitals aren't like museums, with a black-belt curator on every corner. If Mason knew who he was, he'd make one phonecall and within half an hour someone in a white coat would stroll into my brother's room and shove another needle into his arm, or possibly a knife into his throat, and the soul of Cristóbal Baez, delayed for a month, would finally join those of his multi-national forefathers. And very probably that of his sister, unless hers was speeding in the opposite direction.

Still watching me, still unable to comprehend my silence,

still fiddling with that damn drum, Blair said, 'So what do you want – I should take her out and kill her?' He may have been trying to shock me into a response; actually, I think it was a straightforward question to which he required an answer.

Mason had not resumed his seat after his outburst. Now he drifted back towards his desk and perched on its edge. His eyes too were glued to my face. 'Oh, kill her certainly. But I don't think I can allow you to take her away to do it. You've let me down too, remember. I need some earnest of your continued loyalty. Much as it will grieve me, I think I'd better see this.'

Blair's gaze left me to travel over the room, the thick carpets, the heavy curtains, the plush upholstery. 'Here?' Bloodstains in that room would have been quite indelible.

Mason took his point. 'Perhaps not in here, no. Outside somewhere. The covering yard. And a knife, if you please. I trust my staff, but I'd rather there was nothing for them to hear.'

I finally found my voice. It even sounded quite like mine. 'Counting on that, are you?'

From somewhere he dredged up a smile. With it in place he looked quite mad again. And of course he was – quite, quite mad. 'You, of course, will be gagged before you leave this room.'

Like Robespierre, his jaw shattered by a pistol ball, dragged to his death deprived of his one weapon, his clever tongue. Anything I planned on saying I'd better say here.

Still I held my peace. My ears must have twitched visibly with the effort to hear sirens on the river road or the crunch of footsteps on gravel. Somebody had to come soon. Hellfire, somebody ought to be here *now* – unless Chris was dead, or so badly hurt he couldn't communicate what he knew. I hadn't thought his injuries were that bad, but I'm an historian not a physician and if I had known the first thing about medicine maybe I wouldn't have driven away leaving him wrapped in a blanket by a Mexican roadside. Or maybe it would have made no difference. There hadn't seemed to be much choice. Maybe there was none.

Tense as we all were, the sudden movement of Blair's head was somehow shocking. He was still playing with the drum: he was turning the twisted lid in his fingers when his head shot forward as if someone had hit him behind the ear with a cricket bat. Then he went very still, even to his gaze which was fixed on the ruined leather; and after that again he straightened up quite slowly and vented a soft, thoughtful sigh.

Mason said, 'What is it?'

Blair looked up – at me, not Mason. 'She knows.'

I not only didn't know, I didn't even guess. But looking from one to the other of them – Mason mad, bad and as dangerous as weeping gelignite, Blair calm and capable and quite ready to kill me when the moment came – I knew it had to be good news, that absolutely nothing could make my situation worse. I nodded. Then I nodded again, more emphatically. Then I said, 'That's right,' just to make sure.

I'm not generally a bad liar. Trouble is, I lack the big match temperament. I can fluff it when the chips go down. Even before I opened my mouth, a look of doubt had crept across Blair's face. 'They told you?'

'Of course.'

'It didn't worry you?'

As non-committally as I could, I shrugged. 'Some.'

'But you thought we wouldn't find it.'

'Find what?' asked Mason.

Blair was still regarding me with that equivocal gaze, but there was less doubt now, more certainty, and a kind of bemused humour. 'Tell Mr Mason what I've found.'

All right, so anyone with a titter of wit could have guessed. I guessed about 3b's Tarzangram on my birthday and this was a doddle compared with that. I must cope better with threats to my dignity than to my life. I gave up with a bad grace. 'A cat flap. Thirteen elephants in a mangrove swamp. A greenhouse full of cucumbers. How the hell should I know what you've found?'

'She doesn't know,' he said to Mason, a strain of wonder in his voice. 'They've sent her damn near a thousand miles to do a job any reasonable man would kill her for, and they didn't even tell her. They put a wire on her and she never even knew.'

I thought about that. There seemed to be time to think about it. I ended up sharing Blair's rather obvious sense of pity. There was no point in lying any more. 'No,' I said. 'I didn't know about that.'

It was true, as far as it went. It was so patently true they believed without question. And, being true, it dug all the hole they needed to bury me. Blair knew it. I knew it. As I watched Mason, the knowledge spread over his face like a slow dawn. 'You set me up?' he said at last.

I said nothing. There was no percentage in confirming it.

'From the start? From when you first came here and asked for my help, you meant to betray me?' He sounded affronted, outraged, like a man whose hospitality has been abused. 'It was all a – ?' He spread his hand, a small elegant hand, unable to find expression for the depth of his feeling. His eyes, wandering round the room in a state of shock, fell on the debris on the table. 'You risked that – you sacrificed that! – just to hurt me? *Why?*'

Again I shrugged. 'Someone had to stop you. I had the means.' Momentarily I jumped out of my skin at the sudden thump on the floor that was Blair stamping on the little white gismo he had winkled out of the charred lining of the leather lid.

I don't think Mason blinked. 'Why stop me? What harm have I done you?'

I stared at him, unable to comprehend. 'The small matter of my brother?' I prompted incredulously.

'Your brother?' He sounded genuinely perplexed. I

swear that, just for the moment, the bastard had forgotten. 'Oh yes, the half-breed in the back of the truck. He got what was coming to him. He didn't have to take me on, you know. I didn't ask him to ride with us. I'd have paid him to turn a blind eye. People like that just aren't reasonable. What's a businessman to do if the opposition just keeps coming?'

'You killed six men!'

'Seven,' he said, not as if it was a matter of particular pride, just that he liked to keep his figures right. 'Seven is not a lot of lives here. If I went out of business tomorrow, by the end of the month malnutrition and disease would have killed more than seven of the people I am booked to bring up. This is a five-million-monkey-a-year business, and all of them want to come because they can't get a half-decent life in their own country. Their kids are sick all the time. They can't afford what it costs to educate them.

'So they come up here, and hunt round for some place to stay where the landlord will let them keep the kids with them, even though he'll charge them for the privilege, and some place to work where the boss won't tell Immigration when their wages are due.

'And do you know how much harm they do here? None. Not to the labour force, not to the economy. They do work you can't get documented labour to do. They even pay taxes – they pay twenty-five times in taxes what they draw in social security. They're good business to this country. God forbid the government should ever see that, of course, because if they do they'll put me out of a job.'

He gave me a wry, worldly smile for all the world as if I were not the woman he was going to have killed.

Blair had said something that neither Mason nor I, intent on one another, had taken in. Now, patiently, he said it again. 'I said, the wire isn't working now, but there's no way of knowing if it was working after the fire or not.'

Mason looked at him, displeased with the interruption. 'So?'

'So we ought to get out of here.'

Again that note of horror, of outrage. 'This is my home!'

'Jesus Christ,' Blair exploded, 'do you want me to put it to music? This whole thing was set up to get you. It was a trap from the beginning, and it was designed and baited specifically for you. With or without the wire, they know where to find you. If it was working till just now they'll be at the gate. If it quit at the fire, they may wait a few hours to hear from her, but when they don't they'll be in here at first light. We need every minute we can get as a head-start. In these hills, in the dark, I can outrun anyone they send. But if we're not across the border by daylight they'll put up spotter planes and they'll get us.'

'Across the border? What are you talking about? I'm not leaving my home!'

'One way or another, Mr Mason, you're leaving it.' There was no doubt in Blair's face or voice. 'With me, now, or with Cade, soon.'

'They have nothing on me.'

'They *know*. They knew when they set out their stall, when they gave her that wire to carry. You think that was speculation? That – thing – they gave her to bribe you with, it was worth a fortune. They knew they could lose it, but it was worth it to them. It was worth that much to nail you. They've done it. They have you every way but in handcuffs, and if you stay here they'll have you that way too.'

I was just beginning to hope they'd forgotten about me. I was jumping the gun. Mason's eyes, mad with hurt and rage, came back at me with a crack like a whiplash. Incredibly, there were tears in them.

'You,' he cried, and I flinched. 'You did this. You abused my friendship and my trust. You destroyed my codex, and now I'm going to lose my home and all my treasures because of you. All because of some Mexican half-breed whose own father didn't care if he lived or died!'

'Leave her,' said Blair, getting to his feet. 'We have to go.'

'Leave her? Oh no,' said Mason, with conviction.

There was a desk-set on his desk, as on desks everywhere. With the red and black pens, and the neon highlighter, and the stapler, the pencil sharpener and the fancy little brass seal, there was – as with desk-sets everywhere – a paperknife. It was a particularly elegant paperknife, long and slender. Its point, of course, was blunt, its edge unhoned, but all that meant was that, thrust into my body with enough force, it would hurt more than a stiletto, not that it would be less effective. It was plenty long enough to reach my heart from the point of access below my ribs.

I knew that his hand would light on it long before it did. At least, it felt a long time.

Blair shook his head. 'Right now all they can prove is smuggling. You waste her, you move the whole thing up a gear.' He didn't know, of course, that I knew about the Colombian. All in all, now didn't seem a good time to tell him.

'Right now,' spat Mason, 'they can prove nothing. All they have is a witness. Without her there's no case.'

'They *know* – '

'What they know and what they can make stick in court are two very different things. I have good lawyers.'

Like an Apaché dancer, or perhaps more like a picador, lance in hand, he advanced on me, the grace of his body mesmeric, charming like a snake or a mongoose. Blair stood where he was, undecided.

I said, all in a rush, 'My brother isn't dead, he's alive, he was with me in the rig; now he's in a Mexican hospital talking nineteen to the dozen to the local police, and everything I know he knows too.' That's a lot of betrayal in just one sentence.

Mason froze for a moment, then let out all his breath in one long gasp of hatred. 'Oh, you enemy!'

Someone had pulled the chair-trick on Blair. The bottom had dropped out of his face. Finally he said, 'The

Mexican kid. He even said his name was Colón. Cristóbal
Colón, for God's sake!'

'Yes.' I had kicked myself over that, too.

'The one who was hurt in the fire,' he told Mason,
automatically, not because the explanation was necessary.

'I want them dead,' Mason said thickly, as though
through blood. 'You see to the boy when we get down
there, but her I want dead here and now.' He couldn't do it
himself after all, too squeamish or just not knowledgeable
enough.

And it hadn't worked. They were supposed to want all
the details, and to put off killing me while we discussed
them. But they didn't care about the details, they were
going to murder me and then head south to murder Chris.
Blair slowly drew from his belt a heavy hunting-knife, a
hook-backed blade half as broad as my hand. I had run all
out of time.

He moved towards me, less like a snake than a big cat or
a wolf, silent on padded feet, sidling past the table without
sparing it a glance. Like many big, physical men he had an
intense sense of where every part of his body was. Men like
him didn't bump into tables, didn't lose fights.

And as he drew level with Mason he raised the knife
high, hook uppermost, and brought the heavy hilt
crashing down in the angle of his neck and shoulder, and
the rich, clever, evil old man dropped on his own carpet
too quickly even to look surprised. Blood spurting from a
wound left by the rough haft soiled the no doubt priceless
rug.

I found myself looking at Blair, and Blair at me. He
seemed to think an explanation was called for. 'There's
someone coming up the drive. If it's your friends, I don't
want to take a murder rap.'

'What if it's his friends?'

'We'll fight; but we'll probably die.'

We waited. We heard footsteps in the hall, on the stairs.

We heard doors being thrown open, saw the wash of lights springing up all round the house. Finally the study door opened and a revolver came in, followed a moment later by Joshua Cade.

He looked mildly at me, at Blair, at the man on the rug. 'My, you have had a busy day,' he said then.

6

We lined up together to take our medicine – me and Cade and Richard, who looked he'd spent the night at a wake for the codex, alternately crying and drinking – all ranged in front of the big expensive desk. Behind the desk sat the little smiling man whose names boiled down to Esteban Alvarado. Even now he was almost smiling, and serving chocolate from a silver tray. When we each had a cup, and I was trying to work out how to drink without getting the cinnamon stick up my nose, he said gently, 'Tell me what happened.'

So we told him. Mostly I told him, since I had been there throughout and neither of the others had. Chris might have helped, but he was still excused boots in a mission hospital. We were going there when we left here.

And when I had told him, I showed him. After Raoul Mason had been carted away from his precious home to be stitched up and stitched up, I had gone down on my hands and knees with a dust-pan and his Cartier shaving-brush, salvaging all the fragments I could find of that lost treasure. It wasn't that I seriously thought they could be reconstituted, more that I just couldn't leave them there for the next passing vacuum-cleaner. I had put them in a rummer and stretched clingfilm over the top, a combination of the sacred and the profane that afterwards rather amused me. But not yet, not yet.

I put this makeshift snowstorm on his desk. He regarded it wordlessly for some time. Then he said, still quietly, still polite, 'There's someone I'd like you to meet.' He picked up his phone and spoke briefly. I gathered it was a summons, and the party summoned was to bring something with him.

We waited for him in silence. Alvarado tried to top up our chocolate but nobody had drunk enough to make it worthwhile. I stared up at the dreadful chandelier.

In due course there came a tap at the door, to which Alvarado responded. We all looked round in time to see a boy walk in with a big wooden tray. For a moment I thought he was bringing us more bloody chocolate.

I say a boy, though he may have been old enough to vote, to marry without parental consent, even to shave occasionally. He was wearing what had been a white lab coat until he took to decoking boilers in it, and he had four paintbrushes in the breast pocket. Three of them still had paint on them.

He passed shyly between my chair and Richard's, and put the tray on Alvarado's desk. Then he stood and watched in surprise as Richard, whom he probably knew, and I, whom he didn't know from a hole in the wall, went through a strange synchronised ritual best described as formation startling. We looked first at the tray, then at each other, then at Alvarado. I half rose from my chair before sinking back in bewilderment. Richard shot from his as if fired from a gun.

Alvarado waved him back, with calm and courtesy but also quite firmly, like a conductor managing a brilliant but difficult first violin. 'Allow me to present Señor Cande Juárez, who is on loan to us from the Rectorate. He is studying archaeology and conservation, but the remarkable thing about Cande is his skill as an artist. No, not so much an artist – as a forger. He has been copying some of our most important works so that their impact can be enjoyed beyond the confines of a museum case. Such copies are exhibited in regional museums, or loaned for showing abroad, or taken round schools and shown to the children. These are things you would not wish to do with the original item.'

So Cande had copied the codex before Alvarado had lent it to us. I was glad: at least some record remained, other than in flat photographs, of just how marvellous a thing it had been. And it was a very good copy: good enough to make the hurt sting all over again.

Richard said, slowly, 'You unspeakable little bastard' – which I thought was rather rough, the poor kid was only doing what he was told. The boy looked round nervously, clearly wondering where to hide if the English professor came at him with a trowel. But Richard wasn't planning violence, at least not yet. He bent over the tray with his eye just inches above the gloriously coloured fake. And anyway, it wasn't the kid he was abusing.

Alvarado regarded him across the tray, that inscrutable solemn little smile still in situ. 'Yes, my friend?'

'You *bastard*! How could you do this to me? Again! Have you any idea what I've been through? And what about Annie? And what about her brother, who damn near fried trying to save it? *Hijo de puta!* You sod.'

'My friend,' said Alvarado with composure, 'I think you should sit down. You're upset.'

'You're damn right I'm upset! My God, you've made a fool of me again. I'm going to be a laughing-stock from here to the British Museum – the meso-American expert who couldn't tell the difference between a real Mixtec codex and a schoolboy hoax.'

Alvarado took the outburst, as everything else, in his stride. He smiled solemnly at the boy. '*Gracias*, Cande.' Grateful for the dismissal, the kid picked up his tray and left hurriedly.

While he was going Cade leaned over to me and whispered, 'What's going on?'

'I don't know,' I murmured back. But I was beginning to.

Cande Juárez had indeed made a copy of the codex. He

was currently engaged in making a second, because someone had burnt the first one to ashes.

The way Alvarado told it, it made perfect sense. The codex was being worked on when we approached him, the copy almost complete. One last burning of midnight oil and a morning in the drying cabinet and the deceit had been possible.

'But why didn't you tell me?' demanded Richard. 'I've been sweating blood for that thing. Annie risked her life for it.'

'That's why I didn't tell you,' Alvarado explained gently. 'You had to believe it was the real thing. If you had known it was dispensable, sooner or later it would have shown. In the interests of your own safety you had to believe it was the codex. Also, the copy was valuable – I wanted it back. Of course, I didn't anticipate the fire.'

Well no – which of us did? But I was ready to crawl back into those smouldering bales for it, Angel had tried to, and Chris had lost the skin off his back stopping her. We had risked our lives for, and also on the strength of, an essentially worthless copy: if the swap had been suspected, no reasonable man would have given the ashes in the glass on Alvarado's desk for our chances.

And if we had known?

If Richard had known he wouldn't have thrown a wobbly in the Land Rover, and have had to be calmed down with the butt of Chris's gun, which must have gone some way towards convincing Blair's people of our bona fides.

If I had known perhaps the difference would have been evident to Blair when I showed him the thing. Perhaps I would have overplayed my hand, perhaps underplayed it, but somehow struck the false note that would have betrayed us. Certainly I wouldn't have risked anyone's safety to salvage a copy, even a good copy.

Chris would have cheerfully let it burn either way, real or phony, so perhaps it wouldn't have mattered if he had known. But it would have mattered to him if I had given the game away, because they wouldn't have buried me and let him go home. He'd be pushing up the daisies next to mine – or the yuccas or Indian paint-brushes or something – instead of trying to organise a snatch squad to break him out of the Sisters of Mercy. And it would have mattered that Mason and Blair went free.

God damn his eyes, the devious little smiler had been right not to tell us.

And the bug – the little electronic gismo Blair had called a wire?

Joshua Cade dropped his eyes quickly when I raised that other touchy subject, but he wasn't escaping that easily. Alvarado, scrupulously polite, deferred to him for an answer in a way that left no room for speculation.

'Yeah, OK,' he agreed finally, without enthusiasm, 'that was my idea. I didn't like the notion of you disappearing into that desert leaving no tracks. With the wire we could always find where you were.'

'No,' I said carefully, 'with the wire you could always find where the codex was. And if we got split up, for sure the codex would end up with Mason. And that would do almost as well as a live witness, wouldn't it?'

'Well, yes,' he agreed unhappily.

'And it was you, too – wasn't it? – who sent my own brother along as a bodyguard and didn't even tell me he wasn't dead.'

He nodded, resigned. 'Yeah.'

I stood up. He stood up too, hurriedly, almost as if he thought I was going to hit him. I said, still very quietly, 'I think we should leave now, because any moment I'm going to start shouting.'

We made our goodbyes, Alvarado rising, smiling, to shake our hands as we left, Richard glowering into his chocolate, clearly thinking up interesting things to do with a cinnamon stick.

As we closed the big wooden door behind us and took the three paces demanded by convention before I could slam Cade against the wall and launch into a tirade of abuse, there came from within an almighty crash and a clatter, as of a silver tray hitting a crystal chandelier.